THE COLLECTED EDITION OF
THE WORKS OF W. SOMERSET MAUGHAM

LIZA OF LAMBETH

W. SOMERSET MAUGHAM

LIZA OF LAMBETH

★

HEINEMANN : LONDON

William Heinemann Ltd
15 Queen Street, Mayfair, London WIX 8BE

LONDON   MELBOURNE   TORONTO
JOHANNESBURG   AUCKLAND

First Published 1897
New Impressions 1897, 1904, 1906, 1914,
1915, 1918, 1920, 1925
First issued in the Travellers' Library 1930
Collected Edition 1934
New Impressions 1937, 1939, 1950, 1966, 1972, 1976

434 45601 2

St| TF → NC

MADE AND PRINTED IN GREAT BRITAIN BY
MORRISON AND GIBB LIMITED, LONDON AND EDINBURGH

LIZA

OF LAMBETH

CHAPTER I

IT was the first Saturday afternoon in August; it had been broiling hot all day, with a cloudless sky, and the sun had been beating down on the houses, so that the top rooms were like ovens; but now with the approach of evening it was cooler, and everyone in Vere Street was out of doors.

Vere Street, Lambeth, is a short, straight street leading out of the Westminster Bridge Road; it has forty houses on one side and forty houses on the other, and these eighty houses are very much more like one another than ever peas are like peas, or young ladies like young ladies. They are newish, three-storied buildings of dingy grey brick with slate roofs, and they are perfectly flat, without a bow-window or even a projecting cornice or window-sill to break the straightness of the line from one end of the street to the other.

This Saturday afternoon the street was full of life; no traffic came down Vere Street, and the cemented space between the pavements was given up to children. Several games of cricket were being played by wildly excited boys, using coats for wickets, an old tennis-ball or a bundle of rags tied together for a ball, and, generally, an old broomstick for bat. The wicket was so large and the bat so small that the man in was always getting bowled, when heated quarrels would arise, the batter absolutely refusing to go out and the bowler absolutely insisting on going in. The girls were more peaceable; they were chiefly employed in skipping, and only abused one another mildly when the rope was not properly turned or the skipper did not jump sufficiently high. Worst off of all were the very young children, for there had been no rain for weeks, and the street was as dry and clean as a covered court, and, in the lack of mud to wallow in, they sat about the road, disconsolate as poets. The number of babies was prodigious; they sprawled about everywhere, on the pavement, round the doors, and about their mothers' skirts. The grown-ups were gathered round the open doors; there were usually two women squatting on the doorstep, and two or three more seated on either side on chairs; they were invariably nursing babies, and most of them showed clear signs that the present object of the maternal care would be soon ousted by a new arrival. Men were less numerous but such as there were leant against the walls, smoking, or sat on the sills of the ground-floor windows. It was the dead season in Vere Street as much as in Belgravia, and really if it had not been for babies just come or just about to come, and an opportune murder in a neighbouring doss-house, there would have been nothing whatever to talk about. As it was, the little groups talked quietly, discussing the atrocity or the merits of the local midwives, comparing the circumstances of their various confinements.

"You'll be 'avin' your little trouble soon, eh, Polly?" asked one good lady of another.

"Oh, I reckon I've got another two months ter go yet," answered Polly.

"Well," said a third, "I wouldn't 'ave thought you'd go so long by the look of yer!"

"I 'ope you'll have it easier this time, my dear," said a very stout old person, a woman of great importance.

"She said she wasn't goin' to 'ave no more, when the last one come." This remark came from Polly's husband.

"Ah," said the stout old lady, who was in the business, and boasted vast experience. "That's wot they all says; but, Lor' bless yer, they don't mean it."

"Well, I've got three, and I'm not goin' to 'ave no more bli'me if I will; 'tain't good enough—that's wot I says."

"You're abaht right there, ole gal," said Polly. "My word, 'Arry, if you 'ave any more I'll git a divorce, that I will."

At that moment an organ-grinder turned the corner and came down the street.

"Good biz; 'ere's an organ!" cried half a dozen people at once.

The organ-man was an Italian, with a shock of black hair and a ferocious moustache. Drawing his organ to a favourable spot, he stopped, released his shoulder from the leather straps by which he dragged it, and cocking his large soft hat on the side of his head, began turning the handle. It was a lively tune, and in less than no time a little crowd had gathered round to listen, chiefly the young men and the maidens, for the married ladies were never in a fit state to dance, and therefore disinclined to trouble themselves to stand round the organ. There was a moment's hesitation at opening the ball; then one girl said to another:

"Come on, Florrie, you and me ain't shy; we'll begin, and bust it!"

The two girls took hold of one another, one acting gentleman, the other lady; three or four more pairs of girls immediately joined them, and they began a waltz. They held themselves very upright; and with an air of grave dignity which was quite impressive, glided slowly about, making their steps with the utmost precision, bearing themselves with sufficient decorum for a court ball. After a while the men began to itch for a turn, and two of them, taking hold of one another in the most approved fashion, waltzed round the circle with the gravity of judges.

All at once there was a cry: "There's Liza!" And several members of the group turned and called out: "Oo, look at Liza!"

The dancers stopped to see the sight, and the organ-grinder, having come to the end of his tune, ceased turning the handle and looked to see what was the excitement.

"Oo, Liza!" they called out. "Look at Liza; oo, I sy!"

It was a young girl of about eighteen, with dark eyes, and an enormous fringe, puffed-out and curled and frizzed, covering her whole forehead from side to side, and coming down to meet her eyebrows. She was dressed in brilliant violet, with great lappets of velvet, and she had on her head an enormous black hat covered with feathers.

"I sy, ain't she got up dossy?" called out the groups at the doors, as she passed.

"Dressed ter death, and kill the fashion; that's wot I calls it."

4

Liza saw what a sensation she was creating; she arched her back and lifted her head, and walked down the street, swaying her body from side to side, and swaggering along as though the whole place belonged to her.

" 'Ave yer bought the street, Bill?" shouted one youth; and then half a dozen burst forth at once, as if by inspiration:

"Knocked 'em in the Old Kent Road!"

It was immediately taken up by a dozen more, and they all yelled it out:

"Knocked 'em in the Old Kent Road. Yah, ah, knocked 'em in the Old Kent Road!"

"Oo, Liza!" they shouted; the whole street joined in, and they gave long, shrill, ear-piercing shrieks and strange calls, that rung down the street and echoed back again.

"Hextra special!" called out a wag.

"Oh, Liza! Oo! Ooo!" yells and whistles, and then it thundered forth again:

"Knocked 'em in the Old Kent Road!"

Liza put on the air of a conquering hero, and sauntered on, enchanted at the uproar. She stuck out her elbows and jerked her head on one side, and said to herself as she passed through the bellowing crowd:

"This is jam!"

"Knocked 'em in the Old Kent Road!"

When she came to the group round the barrel-organ, one of the girls cried out to her:

"Is that yer new dress, Liza?"

"Well, it don't look like my old one, do it?" said Liza.

"Where did yer git it?" asked another friend, rather enviously.

5

"Picked it up in the street, of course," scornfully answered Liza.

"I believe it's the same one as I saw in the pawnbroker's dahn the road," said one of the men, to tease her.

"Thet's it; but wot was you doin' in there? Pledgin' yer shirt, or was it yer trousers?"

"Yah, I wouldn't git a second-'and dress at a pawnbroker's!"

"Garn!" said Liza indignantly. "I'll swipe yer over the snitch if yer talk ter me. I got the mayterials in the West Hend, didn't I? And I 'ad it mide up by my Court Dressmiker, so you jolly well dry up, old jelly-belly."

"Garn!" was the reply.

Liza had been so intent on her new dress and the comment it was exciting that she had not noticed the organ.

"Oo, I say, let's 'ave some dancin'," she said as soon as she saw it. "Come on, Sally," she added, to one of the girls, "you an' me'll dance togither. Grind away, old cock!"

The man turned on a new tune, and the organ began to play the Intermezzo from the "Cavalleria"; other couples quickly followed Liza's example, and they began to waltz round with the same solemnity as before; but Liza outdid them all; if the otners were as stately as queens, she was as stately as an empress; the gravity and dignity with which she waltzed were something appalling, you felt that the minuet was a frolic in comparison; it would have been a fitting measure to tread round the grave of a *première danseuse*, or at the funeral of a professional humorist. And the graces she put on, the languor of the eyes, the contemptuous curl of the lips, the exquisite turn of the hand, the dainty arching

6

of the foot! You felt there could be no questioning her right to the tyranny of Vere Street.

Suddenly she stopped short, and disengaged herself from her companion.

"Oh, I sy," she said, "this is too bloomin' slow; it gives me the sick."

That is not precisely what she said, but it is impossible always to give the exact unexpurgated words of Liza and the other personages of the story; the reader is therefore entreated with his thoughts to piece out the necessary imperfections of the dialogue.

"It's too bloomin' slow," she said again; "it gives me the sick. Let's 'ave somethin' a bit more lively than this 'ere waltz. You stand over there, Sally, an' we'll show 'em 'ow ter skirt dance."

They all stopped waltzing.

"Talk of the ballet at the Canterbury and the South London. You just wite till you see the ballet at Vere Street, Lambeth— we'll knock 'em!"

She went up to the organ-grinder.

"Na then, Italiano," she said to him, "you buck up; give us a tune that's got some guts in it! See?"

She caught hold of his big hat and squashed it down over his eyes. The man grinned from ear to ear, and, touching the little catch at the side began to play a lively tune such as Liza had asked for.

The men had fallen out, but several girls had put themselves in position, in couples, standing face to face; and immediately the music struck up, they began. They held up their skirts on each side, so as to show their feet, and proceeded to go through the difficult steps and motions of the dance. Liza was right; they could not have done it better in a trained ballet. But the best dancer of them all was Liza; she threw her whole soul into it; forgetting the stiff bearing which she had thought proper to the waltz, and casting of its elaborate graces, she gave herself up entirely to the present pleasure. Gradually the other couples stood aside, so that Liza and Sally were left alone. They paced it carefully, watching each other's steps, and as if by instinct performing corresponding movements, so as to make the whole a thing of symmetry.

"I'm abaht done," said Sally, blowing and puffing. "I've 'ad enough of it."

"Go on, Liza!" cried out a dozen voices when Sally stopped.

She gave no sign of having heard them other than calmly to continue her dance. She glided through the steps, and swayed about, and manipulated her skirt, all with the most charming grace imaginable, then, the music altering, she changed the style of her dancing, her feet moved more quickly, and did not keep so strictly to the ground. She was getting excited at the admiration of the onlookers, and her dance grew wilder and more daring. She lifted her skirts higher, brought in new and more difficult movements into her improvisation, kicking up her legs she did the wonderful twist, backwards and forwards, of which the dancer is proud.

"Look at 'er legs!" cried one of the men.

"Look at 'er stockin's!" shouted another; and indeed they were remarkable, for Liza had chosen them of the same brilliant hue as her dress, and was herself most proud of the harmony.

8

Her dance became gayer: her feet scarcely touched the ground, she whirled round madly.

"Tike care yer don't split!" cried out one of the wags, at a very audacious kick.

The words were hardly out of his mouth when Liza, with a gigantic effort, raised her foot and kicked off his hat. The feat was greeted with applause, and she went on, making turns and twists, flourishing her skirts, kicking higher and higher, and finally, among a volley of shouts, fell on her hands and turned head over heels in a magnificent catharine-wheel; then scrambling to her feet again, she tumbled into the arms of a young man standing in the front of the ring.

"That's right, Liza," he said. "Give us a kiss, now," and promptly tried to take one.

"Git aht!" said Liza, pushing him away, not too gently.

"Yus, give us a kiss," cried another, running up to her.

"I'll smack yer in the fice!" said Liza, elegantly, as she dodged him.

"Ketch 'old on 'er, Bill," cried out a third, "an' we'll all kiss her."

"Na, you won't!" shrieked Liza, beginning to run.

"Come on," they cried, "we'll ketch 'er."

She dodged in and out, between their legs, under their arms, and then, getting clear of the little crowd, caught up her skirts so that they might not hinder her, and took to her heels along the street. A score of men set in chase, whistling, shouting, yelling; the people at the doors looked up to see the fun, and cried out to her as she dashed past; she ran like the wind. Suddenly a man from the side darted into the middle of the road, stood straight in her way, and before she knew

9

where she was, she had jumped shrieking into his arms, and he, lifting her up to him, had imprinted two sounding kisses on her cheeks.

"Oh, you——!" she said. Her expression was quite unprintable; nor can it be euphemised.

There was a shout of laughter from the bystanders, and the young men in chase of her, and Liza, looking up, saw a big, bearded man whom she had never seen before. She blushed to the very roots of her hair, quickly extricated herself from his arms, and, amid the jeers and laughter of everyone, slid into the door of the nearest house and was lost to view.

CHAPTER II

LIZA and her mother were having supper. Mrs. Kemp was an elderly woman, short, and rather stout, with a red face, and grey hair brushed tight back over her forehead. She had been a widow for many years, and since her husband's death had lived with Liza in the ground-floor front room in which they were now sitting. Her husband had been a soldier, and from a grateful country she received a pension large enough to keep her from starvation, and by charing and doing such odd jobs as she could get she earned a little extra to supply herself with liquor. Liza was able to make her own living by working at a factory.

Mrs. Kemp was rather sulky this evening.

"Wot was yer doin' this afternoon, Liza?" she asked.

"I was in the street."

"You're always in the street when I want yer."

"I didn't know as 'ow yer wanted me, mother," answered Liza.

"Well, yer might 'ave come ter see! I might 'ave been dead, for all you knew."

Liza said nothing.

"My rheumatics was thet bad to-dy, thet I didn't know wot ter do with myself. The doctor said I was to be rubbed with that stuff 'e give me, but yer won't never do nothin' for me."

"Well, mother," said Liza, "your rheumatics was all right yesterday."

"I know wot you was doin'; you was showin' off thet new dress of yours. Pretty waste of money thet is, instead of givin' it me ter sive up. An' for the matter of thet, I wanted a

11

new dress far worse than you did. But, of course, I don't matter."

Liza did not answer, and Mrs. Kemp, having nothing more to say, continued her supper in silence.

It was Liza who spoke next.

"There's some new people moved in the street. 'Ave you seen 'em?" she asked.

"No, wot are they?"

"I dunno; I've seen a chap, a big chap with a beard. I think 'e lives up at the other end."

She felt herself blushing a little.

"No one any good you be sure," said Mrs. Kemp. "I can't swaller these new people as are comin' in; the street ain't wot it was when I fust come."

When they had done, Mrs. Kemp got up, and having finished her half-pint of beer, said to her daughter:

"Put the things awy, Liza. I'm just goin' round to see Mrs. Clayton; she's just 'ad twins, and she 'ad nine before these come. It's a pity the Lord don't see fit ter tike some on 'em—thet's wot I say."

After which pious remark Mrs. Kemp went out of the house and turned into another a few doors up.

Liza did not clear the supper things away as she was told, but opened the window and drew her chair to it. She leant on the sill, looking out into the street. The sun had set, and it was twilight, the sky was growing dark, bringing to view the twinkling stars; there was no breeze, but it was pleasantly and restfully cool. The good folk still sat at their doorsteps, talking as before on the same inexhaustible subjects, but a little subdued with the approach of night. The boys were still playing cricket, but they were mostly at the other end of the street, and their shouts were muffled before they reached Liza's ears.

She sat, leaning her head on her hands, breathing in the fresh air and feeling a certain exquisite sense of peacefulness which she was not used to. It was Saturday evening, and she thankfully remembered that there would be no factory on the morrow; she was glad to rest. Somehow she felt a little tired, perhaps it was through the excitement of the afternoon, and she enjoyed the quietness of the evening. It seemed so tranquil and still; the silence filled her with a strange delight, she felt as if she could sit there all through the night looking out into the cool, dark street, and up heavenwards at the stars. She was very happy, but yet at the same time experienced a strange new sensation of melancholy, and she almost wished to cry.

Suddenly a dark form stepped in front of the open window. She gave a little shriek.

" 'Oo's thet?" she asked, for it was quite dark, and she did not recognise the man standing in front of her.

"Me, Liza," was the answer.

"Tom?"

"Yus!"

It was a young man with light yellow hair and a little fair moustache, which made him appear almost boyish; he was light-complexioned and blue-eyed, and had a frank and pleasant look mingled with a curious bashfulness that made him blush when people spoke to him.

"Wot's up?" asked Liza.

"Come aht for a walk, Liza, will yer?"

13

"No!" she answered decisively.

"You promised ter yesterday, Liza."

"Yesterday an' ter-day's two different things," was her wise reply.

"Yus, come on, Liza."

"Na, I tell yer, I won't."

"I want ter talk ter yer, Liza." Her hand was resting on the window-sill, and he put his upon it. She quickly drew it back.

"Well, I don't want yer ter talk ter me."

But she did, for it was she who broke the silence.

"Say, Tom, 'oo are them new folk as 'as come into the street? It's a big chap with a brown beard."

"D'you mean the bloke as kissed yer this afternoon?"

Liza blushed again

"Well, why shouldn't 'e kiss me?" she said, with some inconsequence.

"I never said as 'ow 'e shouldn't; I only arst yer if it was the sime."

"Yes, thet's 'oo I mean."

" 'Is nime is Blakeston—Jim Blakeston. I've only spoke to 'im once; he's took the two top rooms at No. 19 'ouse."

"Wot's 'e want two top rooms for?"

" 'Im? Oh, 'e's got a big family—five kids. Ain't yer seen 'is wife abaht the street? She's a big, fat woman, as does 'er 'air funny."

"I didn't know 'e 'ad a wife."

There was another silence; Liza sat thinking, and Tom stood at the window, looking at her.

"Won't yer come aht with me, Liza?" he asked, at last.

"Na, Tom," she said, a little more gently, "it's too lite."

14

"Liza," he said, blushing to the roots of his hair.

"Well?"

"Liza"—he couldn't go on, and stuttered in his shyness—"Liza, I—I—I loves yer, Liza."

"Garn awy!"

He was quite brave now, and took hold of her hand.

"Yer know, Liza, I'm earnin' twenty-three shillin's at the works now, an' I've got some furniture as mother left me when she was took."

The girl said nothing.

"Liza, will you 'ave me? I'll make yer a good 'usband, Liza, swop me bob, I will; an' yer know I'm not a drinkin' sort. Liza, will yer marry me?"

"Na, Tom," she answered quietly.

"Oh, Liza, won't you 'ave me?"

"Na, Tom, I can't."

"Why not? You've come aht walkin' with me ever since Whitsun."

"Ah, things is different now."

"You're not walkin' aht with anybody else, are you, Liza?" he asked quickly.

"Na, not that."

"Well, why won't yer, Liza? Oh Liza, I do love yer, I've never loved anybody as I love you!"

"Oh, I can't, Tom!"

"There ain't no one else?"

"Na."

"Then why not?"

"I'm very sorry, Tom, but I don't love yer so as ter marry yer."

"Oh, Liza!"

She could not see the look upon his face, but she heard the agony in his voice; and, moved with sudden pity, she bent out. threw her arms round his neck, and kissed him on both cheeks.

"Never mind old chap!" she said. "I'm not worth troublin' abaht."

And quickly drawing back, she slammed the window to, and moved into the further part of the room.

CHAPTER III

THE following day was Sunday. Liza when she was dressing herself in the morning, felt the hardness of fate in the impossibility of eating one's cake and having it; she wished she had reserved her new dress, and had still before her the sensation of a first appearance in it. With a sigh she put on her ordinary everyday working dress, and proceeded to get the breakfast ready, for her mother had been out late the previous night, celebrating the new arrivals in the street, and had the "rheumatics" this morning.

"Oo, my 'ead!" she was saying, as she pressed her hands on each side of her forehead. "I've got the neuralgy again, wot shall I do? I dunno 'ow it is, but it always comes on Sunday mornings. Oo, an' my rheumatics, they give me sich a doin' in the night!"

"You'd better go to the 'orspital, mother."

"Not I!" answered the worthy lady, with great decision. "You 'as a dozen young chaps messin' you abaht, and lookin' at yer; and then they tells yer ter leave off beer and spirrits. Well, wot I says, I says I can't do withaht my glass of beer." She thumped her pillow to emphasise the statement.

"Wot with the work I 'ave ter do, lookin' after you and the cookin' and gettin' everythin' ready and doin' all the 'ouse-work, and goin' aht charring besides—well, I says, if I don't 'ave a drop of beer, I says, ter pull me together, I should be under the turf in no time."

She munched her bread-and-butter and drank her tea.

"When you've done breakfast, Liza," she said, "you can give the grate a cleanin', an' my boots'd do with a bit of

17

polishin'. Mrs. Tike, in the next 'ouse, 'll give yer some blackin'."

She remained silent for a bit, then said:

"I don't think I shall get up ter-day, Liza. My rheumatics is bad. You can put the room straight and cook the dinner."

"Arright, mother; you stay where you are, an' I'll do everythin' for yer."

"Well, it's only wot yer ought to do, considerin' all the trouble you've been ter me when you was young, and considerin' thet when you was born the doctor thought I never should get through it. Wot 'ave you done with your week's money, Liza?"

"Oh, I've put it awy," answered Liza quietly.

"Where?" asked her mother.

"Where it'll be safe."

"Where's that?"

Liza was driven into a corner.

"Why d'you want ter know?" she asked.

"Why shouldn't I know; d'you think I want ter steal it from yer?"

"Na, not thet."

"Well, why won't you tell me?"

"Oh, a thing's sifer when only one person knows where it is."

This was a very discreet remark, but it set Mrs. Kemp in a whirlwind of passion. She raised herself and sat up in the bed, flourishing her clenched fist at her daughter.

"I know wot yer mean, you—you!" Her language was emphatic, her epithets picturesque, but too forcible for reproduction. "You think I'd steal it," she went on. "I know yer! D'yer think I'd go an' tike yer dirty money?"

18

"Well, mother," said Liza, "when I've told yer before, the money's perspired like."

"Wot d'yer mean?"

"It got less."

"Well, I can't 'elp thet, can I? Anyone can come in 'ere and tike the money."

"If it's 'idden awy, they can't, can they, mother?" said Liza.

Mrs. Kemp shook her fist.

"You dirty slut, you," she said, "yer think I tike yer money! Why, you ought ter give it me every week instead of savin' it up and spendin' it on all sorts of muck, while I 'ave ter grind my very bones down to keep yer."

"Yer know, mother, if I didn't 'ave a little bit saved up, we should be rather short when you're dahn in yer luck."

Mrs. Kemp's money always ran out on Tuesday, and Liza had to keep things going till the following Saturday.

"Oh, don't talk ter me!" proceeded Mrs. Kemp. "When I was a girl I give all my money ter my mother. She never 'ad ter ask me for nothin'. On Saturday when I come 'ome with my wiges, I give it 'er every farthin'. That's wot a daughter ought ter do. I can say this for myself, I be'aved by my mother like a gal should. None of your prodigal sons for me! She didn't 'ave ter ask me for three 'apence ter get a drop of beer."

Liza was wise in her generation; she held her tongue, and put on her hat.

"Now, you're goin' aht, and leavin' me; I dunno wot you get up to in the street with all those men. No good, I'll be bound. An' 'ere am I left all alone, an' I might die for all you care."

In her sorrow at herself the old lady began to cry, and Liza slipped out of the room and into the street.

Leaning against the wall of the opposite house was Tom; he came towards her.

" 'Ulloa!" she said, as she saw him. "Wot are you doin' 'ere?"

"I was waitin' for you ter come aht, Liza," he answered.

She looked at him quickly.

"I ain't comin' aht with yer ter-day, if thet's wot yer mean," she said.

"I never thought of arskin' yer, Liza—after wot you said ter me last night."

His voice was a little sad, and she felt so sorry for him.

"But yer did want ter speak ter me, didn't yer, Tom?" she said, more gently.

"You've got a day off ter-morrow, ain't yer?"

"Bank 'Oliday. Yus! Why?"

"Why, 'cause they've got a drag startin' from the 'Red Lion' that's goin' down ter Chingford for the day—an' I'm goin'."

"Yus!" she said.

He looked at her doubtfully.

"Will yer come too, Liza? It'll be a regular beeno; there's only goin' ter be people in the street. Eh, Liza?"

"Na, I can't."

"Why not?"

"I ain't got—I ain't got the ooftish."

"I mean, won't yer come with me?"

"Na, Tom, thank yer; I can't do thet neither."

"Yer might as well, Liza; it wouldn't 'urt yer."

20

"Na, it wouldn't be right like; I can't come aht with yer, and then mean nothin'! It would be doin' yer aht of an outing."

"I don't see why," he said, very crestfallen.

"I can't go on keepin' company with you—after what I said last night."

"I shan't enjoy it a bit without you, Liza."

"You git somebody else, Tom. You'll do withaht me all right."

She nodded to him. and walked up the street to the house of her friend Sally. Having arrived in front of it, she put her hands to her mouth in trumpet form, and shouted:

" 'I! 'I! 'I! Sally!"

A couple of fellows standing by copied her.

" 'I! 'I! 'I! Sally!"

"Garn!" said Liza, looking round at them.

Sally did not appear and she repeated her call. The men imitated her, and half a dozen took it up, so that there was enough noise to wake the seven sleepers.

" 'I! 'I! 'I! Sally!"

A head was put out of a top window, and Liza, taking off her hat, waved it, crying:

"Come on dahn, Sally!"

"Arright, old gal!" shouted the other. "I'm comin'!"

"So's Christmas!" was Liza's repartee.

There was a clatter down the stairs, and Sally, rushing through the passage, threw herself on to her friend. They began fooling, in reminiscence of a melodrama they had lately seen together.

"Oh, my darlin' duck!" said Liza, kissing her and pressing her, with affected rapture, to her bosom.

21

"My sweetest sweet!" replied Sally, copying her.

"An' 'ow does your lidyship ter-day?"

"Oh!"—with immense languor—"fust class; and is your royal 'ighness quite well?"

"I deeply regret," answered Liza, "but my royal 'ighness 'as got the collywobbles."

Sally was a small, thin girl, with sandy hair and blue eyes, and a very freckled complexion. She had an enormous mouth, with terrible, square teeth set wide apart, which looked as if they could masticate an iron bar. She was dressed like Liza, in a shortish black skirt and an old-fashioned bodice, green and grey and yellow with age; her sleeves were tucked up to the elbow, and she wore a singularly dirty apron, that had once been white.

"Wot 'ave you got yer 'air in them things for?" asked Liza, pointing to the curl-papers. "Goin' aht with yer young man ter-day?"

"No, I'm going ter stay 'ere all day."

"Wot for, then?"

"Why, 'Arry's going ter tike me ter Chingford ter-morrer."

"Oh? In the 'Red Lion' brake?"

"Yus. Are you goin'?"

"Na!"

"Not! Well, why don't you get round Tom? 'E'll tike yer, and jolly glad 'e'll be, too."

" 'E arst me ter go with 'im, but I wouldn't."

"Swop me bob—why not?"

"I ain't keepin' company with 'im."

"Yer might 'ave gone with 'im all the sime."

"Na. You're goin' with 'Arry, ain't yer?"

"Yus!"

"An' you're goin' to 'ave 'im?"

"Right again!"

"Well, I couldn't go with Tom, an' then throw 'im over."

"Well, you are a mug!"

The two girls had strolled down towards the Westminster Bridge Road, and Sally, meeting her young man, had gone to him. Liza walked back, wishing to get home in time to cook the dinner. But she went slowly, for she knew every dweller in the street, and as she passed the groups sitting at their doors, as on the previous evening, but this time mostly engaged in peeling potatoes or shelling peas, she stopped and had a little chat. Everyone liked her, and was glad to have her company. "Good old Liza," they would say, as she left them, "she's a rare good sort, ain't she?"

She asked after the aches and pains of all the old people, and delicately inquired after the babies, past and future; the children hung on to her skirts and asked her to play with them, and she would hold one end of the rope while tiny little ragged girls skipped, invariably entangling themselves after two jumps.

She had nearly reached home, when she heard a voice cry:

"Mornin'!"

She looked round and recognised the man whom Tom had told her was called Jim Blakeston. He was sitting on a stool at the door of one of the houses, playing with two young children, to whom he was giving rides on his knee. She remembered his 'ieavy brown beard from the day before, and she had also an mpression of great size; she noticed this morning that he was, in fact, a big man, tall and broad, and she saw besides that he had large, masculine features and pleasant brown eyes. She supposed him to be about forty.

"Mornin'!" he said again, as she stopped and looked at him.

Liza blushed scarlet, and was too confused to answer.

"Well, yer needn't look as if I was goin' ter eat yer up, 'cause I ain't," he said.

" 'Oo are you? I'm not afeard of yer."

"Wot are yer so bloomin' red abaht?" he asked pointedly.

"Well, I'm 'ot."

"You ain't shirty 'cause I kissed yer last night?"

"I'm not shirty; but it was pretty cool, considerin' like as I didn't know yer."

"Well, you run into my arms."

"Thet I didn't; you run aht and caught me."

"An' kissed yer before you could say 'Jack Robinson'." He laughed at the thought. "Well, Liza," he went on, "seein' as 'ow I kissed yer against yer will, the best thing you can do ter make it up is to kiss me not against yer will."

"Me?" said Liza, looking at him, open-mouthed. "Well you are a pill!"

The children began to clamour for the riding, which had been discontinued on Liza's approach.

"Are them your kids?" she asked.

"Yus; them's two on 'em."

" 'Ow many 'ave yer got?"

"Five; the eldest gal's fifteen, and the next one 'oo's a boy's twelve, and then there are these two and baby."

"Well, you've got enough for your money."

"Too many for me—and more comin'."

24

"Ah, well," said Liza, laughing, "thet's your fault, ain't it?"

Then she bade him good morning, and strolled off.

He watched her as she went, and saw half a dozen little boys surround her and beg her to join them in their game of cricket. They caught hold of her arms and skirts, and pulled her to their pitch.

"Na, I can't," she said, trying to disengage herself. "I've got the dinner ter cook."

"Dinner ter cook?" shouted one small boy. "Why, they always cooks the cats' meat at the shop."

"You little so-and-so!" said Liza, somewhat inelegantly, making a dash at him.

He dodged her and gave a whoop; then turning he caught her round the legs, and another boy catching hold of her round the neck they dragged her down, and all three struggled on the ground, rolling over and over; the other boys threw themselves on the top, so that there was a great heap of legs and arms and heads waving and bobbing up and down.

Liza extricated herself with some difficulty, and taking off her hat she began cuffing the boys with it, using all the time the most lively expressions. Then, having cleared the field, she retired victorious into her own house and began cooking the dinner.

CHAPTER IV

BANK HOLIDAY was a beautiful day: the cloudless sky threatened a stifling heat for noontide, but early in the morning, when Liza got out of bed and threw open the window, it was fresh and cool. She dressed herself, wondering how she should spend her day; she thought of Sally going off to Chingford with her lover, and of herself remaining alone in the dull street with half the people away. She almost wished it were an ordinary work-day, and that there were no such things as bank holidays. And it seemed to be a little like two Sundays running, but with the second rather worse than the first. Her mother was still sleeping, and she was in no great hurry about getting the breakfast, but stood quietly looking out of the window at the house opposite.

In a little while she saw Sally coming along. She was, arrayed in purple and fine linen—a very smart red dress, trimmed with velveteen, and a tremendous hat covered with feathers. She had reaped the benefit of keeping her hair in curl-papers since Saturday, and her sandy fringe stretched from ear to ear. She was in enormous spirits.

" 'Ulloa, Liza!" she called as soon as she saw her at the window.

Liza looked at her a little enviously.

" 'Ulloa!" she answered quietly.

"I'm just goin' to the 'Red Lion' to meet 'Arry."

"At what time d'yer start?"

"The brake leaves at 'alf-past eight sharp."

"Why, it's only eight; it's only just struck at the church. 'Arry won't be there yet, will he?"

"Oh, 'e's sure ter be early. I couldn't wite. I've been witin' abaht since 'alf-past six. I've been up since five this morning."

"Since five! What 'ave you been doin'?"

"Dressin' myself and doin' my 'air. I woke up so early. I've been dreamin' all the night abaht it. I simply couldn't sleep."

"Well, you are a caution!" said Liza.

"Bust it, I don't go on the spree every day! Oh, I do 'ope I shall enjoy myself."

"Why, you simply dunno where you are!" said Liza, a little crossly.

"Don't you wish you was comin', Liza?" asked Sally.

"Na! I could if I liked, but I don't want ter."

"You are a coughdrop—thet's all I can say. Ketch me refusin' when I 'ave the chanst."

"Well, it's done now. I ain't got the chanst any more." Liza said this with just a little regret in her voice.

"Come on dahn to the 'Red Lion', Liza, and see us off," said Sally.

"No, I'm damned if I do!" answered Liza, with some warmth.

"You might as well. P'raps 'Arry won't be there, an' you can keep me company till 'e comes   An' you can see the 'orses."

Liza was really very anxious to see the brake and the horses and the people going; but she hesitated a little longer. Sally asked her once again. Then she said:

"Arright; I'll come with yer, and wite till the bloomin' old thing starts."

She did not trouble to put on a hat, but just walked out as

she was, and accompanied Sally to the public-house which was getting up the expedition.

Although there was still nearly half an hour to wait, the brake was drawn up before the main entrance; it was large and long, with seats arranged crosswise, so that four people could sit on each; and it was drawn by two powerful horses, whose harness the coachman was now examining. Sally was not the first on the scene, for already half a dozen people had taken their places, but Harry had not yet arrived. The two girls stood by the public-door, looking at the preparations. Huge baskets full of food were brought out and stowed away; cases of beer were hoisted up and put in every possible place—under the seats, under the driver's legs, and even beneath the brake As more people came up, Sally began to get excited about Harry's non-appearance.

"I say, I wish 'e'd come!" she said. " 'E is lite."

Then she looked up and down the Westminster Bridge Road to see if he was in view.

"Suppose 'e don't turn up! I will give it 'im when 'e comes for keepin' me witin' like this."

"Why, there's a quarter of an hour yet," said Liza, who saw nothing at all to get excited about.

At last Sally saw her lover, and rushed off to meet him. Liza was left alone, rather disconsolate at all this bustle and preparation. She was not sorry that she had refused Tom's invitation, but she did wish that she had conscientiously been able to accept it. Sally and her friend came up; attired in his Sunday best, he was a fit match for his lady-love—he wore a shirt and collar, unusual luxuries—and he carried under his arm a concertina to make things merry on the way.

"Ain't you goin', Liza?" he asked in surprise at seeing her without a hat and with her apron on.

"Na," said Sally, "ain't she a soft? Tom said 'e'd tike 'er, an' she wouldn't."

"Well, I'm dashed!"

Then they climbed the ladder and took their seats, so that Liza was left alone again. More people had come along, and the brake was nearly full. Liza knew them all, but they were too busy taking their places to talk to her. At last Tom came. He saw her standing there and went up to her.

"Won't yer change yer mind, Liza, an' come along with us?"

"Na, Tom, I told yer I wouldn't—it's not right like." She felt she must repeat that to herself often.

"I shan't enjoy it a bit without you," he said.

"Well, I can't 'elp it!" she answered, somewhat sullenly.

At that moment a man came out of the public-house with a horn in his hand; her heart gave a great jump, for if there was anything she adored it was to drive along to the tootling of a horn. She really felt it was very hard lines that she must stay at home when all these people were going to have such a fine time; and they were all so merry, and she could picture to herself so well the delights of the drive and the picnic. She felt very much inclined to cry. But she mustn't go, and she wouldn't go: she repeated that to herself twice as the trumpeter gave a preliminary tootle.

Two more people hurried along, and when they came near Liza saw that they were Jim Blakeston and a woman whom she supposed to be his wife.

"Are you comin' Liza?" Jim said to her.

"No," she answered. "I didn't know you was goin'."

"I wish you was comin'," he replied, "we shall 'ave a game."

She could only just keep back the sobs; she so wished she were going. It did seem hard that she must remain behind; and all because she wasn't going to marry Tom. After all, she didn't see why that should prevent her; there really was no need to refuse for that. She began to think she had acted foolishly: it didn't do anyone any good that she refused to go out with Tom, and no one thought it anything specially fine that she should renounce her pleasure. Sally merely thought her a fool.

Tom was standing by her side, silent, and looking disappointed and rather unhappy. Jim said to her, in a low voice:

"I am sorry you're not comin'!"

It was too much. She did want to go so badly, and she really couldn't resist any longer. If Tom would only ask her once more, and if she could only change her mind reasonably and decently, she would accept; but he stood silent, and she had to speak herself. It was very undignified.

"Yer know, Tom," she said, "I don't want ter spoil your day."

"Well, I don't think I shall go alone; it 'ud be so precious slow."

Supposing he didn't ask her again! What should she do? She looked up at the clock on the front of the pub, and noticed that it only wanted five minutes to the half-hour. How terrible it would be if the brake started and he didn't ask her! Her heart beat violently against her chest, and in her agitation she fumbled with the corner of her apron.

30

"Well, what can I do, Tom dear?"

'Why, come with me, of course. Oh, Liza, do say yes."

She had got the offer again, and it only wanted a little seemly hesitation, and the thing was done.

"I should like ter, Tom," she said. "But d'you think it 'ud be arright?"

"Yus, of course it would. Come on, Liza!" In his eagerness he clasped her hand.

"Well," she remarked, looking down, "if it'd spoil your 'oliday——"

"I won't go if you don't—swop me bob, I won't!" he answered.

"Well, if I come, it won't mean that I'm keepin' company with you."

"Na, it won't mean anythin' you don't like."

"Arright!" she said.

"You'll come?" he could hardly believe her.

"Yus!" she answered, smiling all over her face.

"You're a good sort, Liza! I say, 'Arry, Liza's comin'!" he shouted.

"Liza? 'Oorray!" shouted Harry.

" 'S'at right, Liza?" called Sally.

And Liza feeling quite joyful and light of heart called back: "Yus!"

" 'Oorray!" shouted Sally in answer.

"Thet's right, Liza," called Jim; and he smiled pleasantly as she looked at him.

"There's just room for you two 'ere," said Harry, pointing to the vacant places by his side.

"Arright!" said Tom.

"I must jest go an' get a 'at an' tell mother," said Liza.

"There's just three minutes. Be quick!" answered Tom, and as she scampered off as hard as she could go, he shouted to the coachman: " 'Old 'ard; there's another passenger comin' in a minute."

"Arright, old cock," answered the coachman; "no 'urry!"

Liza rushed into the room, and called to her mother, who was still asleep:

"Mother! mother! I'm going to Chingford!"

Then tearing off her old dress she slipped into her gorgeous violet one; she kicked off her old ragged shoes and put on her new boots. She brushed her hair down and rapidly gave her fringe a twirl and a twist—it was luckily still moderately in curl from the previous Saturday—and putting on her black hat with all the feathers, she rushed along the street, and scrambling up the brake steps fell panting on Tom's lap.

The coachman cracked his whip, the trumpeter tootled his horn, and with a cry and a cheer from the occupants, the brake clattered down the road.

CHAPTER V

AS soon as Liza had recovered herself she started examining the people on the brake; and first of all she took stock of the woman whom Jim Blakeston had with him.

"This is my missus!" said Jim, pointing to her with his thumb.

"You ain't been dahn in the street much, 'ave yer?" said Liza, by way of making the acquaintance.

"Na," answered Mrs. Blakeston, "my youngster's been dahn with the measles, an' I've 'ad my work cut out lookin' after 'im."

"Oh, an' is 'e all right now?"

"Yus, 'e's gettin' on fine, an' Jim wanted ter go ter Chingford ter-day, an' 'e says ter me, well, 'e says, 'You come along ter Chingford, too; it'll do you good.' An' 'e says, 'You can leave Polly'—she's my eldest, yer know—'you can leave Polly,' says 'e, 'ter look after the kids.' So I says, 'Well, I don't mind if I do,' says I."

Meanwhile Liza was looking at her. First she noticed her dress: she wore a black cloak and a funny, old-fashioned black bonnet; then examining the woman herself, she saw a middle-sized, stout person anywhere between thirty and forty years old. She had a large, fat face with a big mouth, and her hair was curiously done, parted in the middle and plastered down on each side of the head in little plaits. One could see that she was a woman of great strength, notwithstanding evident traces of hard work and much child-bearing.

Liza knew all the other passengers, and now that everyone was settled down and had got over the excitement of

33

departure, they had time to greet one another. They were delighted to have Liza among them, for where she was there was no dullness. Her attention was first of all taken up by a young coster who had arrayed himself in the traditional costume—grey suit, tight trousers, and shiny buttons in profusion.

"Wot cheer, Bill!" she cried to him.

"Wot cheer, Liza!" he answered.

"You are got up dossy; you'll knock 'em."

"Na then, Liza Kemp," said his companion, turning round with mock indignation, "you let my Johnny alone. If you come gettin' round 'im I'll give you wot for."

"Arright, Clary Sharp, I don't want 'im," answered Liza. "I've got one of my own, an' thet's a good 'andful—ain't it, Tom?"

Tom was delighted, and, unable to find a repartee, in his pleasure gave Liza a great nudge with his elbow.

" 'Oo, I say," said Liza, putting her hand to her side. "Tike care of my ribs; you'll brike 'em."

"Them's not yer ribs," shouted a candid friend—"them's yer whale-bones yer afraid of breakin'."

"Garn!"

" 'Ave yer got whale-bones?" said Tom, with affected simplicity, putting his arm round her waist to feel.

"Na then," she said, "keep off the grass!"

"Well, I only wanted ter know if you'd got any."

"Garn; yer don't git round me like thet."

He still kept as he was.

"Na then," she repeated, "tike yer 'and away. If yer touch me there you'll 'ave ter marry me."

"Thet's just wot I wants ter do, Liza!"

"Shut it!" she answered cruelly, and drew his arm away from her waist.

The horses scampered on, and the man behind blew his horn with vigour.

"Don't bust yerself, guv'nor!" said one of the passengers to him when he made a particularly discordant sound. They drove along eastwards, and as the hour grew later the streets became more filled and the traffic greater. At last they got on the road to Chingford, and caught up numbers of other vehicles going in the same direction—donkey-shays, pony-carts, tradesmen's carts, dog-carts, drags, brakes, every conceivable kind of wheel thing, all filled with people, the wretched donkey dragging along four solid rate-payers to the pair of stout horses easily managing a couple of score. They exchanged cheers and greetings as they passed, the "Red Lion" brake being noticeable above all for its uproariousness. As the day wore on the sun became hotter, and the road seemed more dusty and threw up a greater heat.

"I am getting 'ot!" was the common cry, and everyone began to puff and sweat.

The ladies removed their cloaks and capes, and the men, following their example, took off their coats and sat in their shirt-sleeves. Whereupon ensued much banter of a not particularly edifying kind respecting the garments which each person would like to remove—which showed that the innuendo of French farce is not so unknown to the upright, honest Englishman as might be supposed.

At last came in sight the half-way house, where the horses were to have a rest and a sponge down. They had been talking

35

of it for the last quarter of a mile, and when at length it was observed on the top of a hill a cheer broke out, and some thirsty wag began to sing "Rule Britannia", whilst others burst forth with a different national ditty, "Beer, Glorious Beer!" They drew up before the pub entrance, and all climbed down as quickly as they could. The bar was besieged, and potmen and barmaids were quickly busy drawing beer and handing it over to the eager folk outside.

The Idyll of Corydon and Phyllis.

Gallantry ordered that the faithful swain and the amorous shepherdess should drink out of one and the same pot.

" 'Urry up an' 'ave your whack," said Corydon, politely handing the foaming bowl for his fair one to drink from.

Phyllis, without replying, raised it to her lips and drank deep. The swain watched anxiously.

" 'Ere, give us a chanst!" he said, as the pot was raised higher and higher and its contents appeared to be getting less and less.

At this the amorous shepherdess stopped and handed the pot to her lover.

"Well, I'm dashed!" said Corydon, looking into it; and added: "I guess you know a thing or two." Then with courtly grace putting his own lips to the place where had been those of his beloved, finished the pint.

"Go' lumme!" remarked the shepherdess, smacking her lips, "that was somethin' like!" And she put out her tongue and licked her lips, and then breathed deeply.

The faithful swain having finished, gave a long sigh, and said:

36

"Well, I could do with some more!"

"For the matter of thet, I could do with a gargle!"

Thus encouraged, the gallant returned to the bar, and soon brought out a second pint.

"You 'ave fust pop," amorously remarked Phyllis, and he took a long drink and handed the pot to her.

She, with maiden modesty, turned it so as to have a different part to drink from; but he remarked as he saw her:

"You are bloomin' particular."

Then, unwilling to grieve him, she turned it back again and applied her ruby lips to the place where his had been.

"Now we shan't be long!" she remarked, as she handed him back the pot.

The faithful swain took out of his pocket a short clay pipe, blew through it, filled it, and began to smoke, while Phyllis sighed at the thought of the cool liquid gliding down her throat, and with the pleasing recollection gently stroked her stomach. Then Corydon spat, and immediately his love said:

"I can spit farther than thet."

"I bet yer yer can't."

She tried, and did. He collected himself and spat again, further than before, she followed him, and in this idyllic contest they remained till the tootling horn warned them to take their places.

At last they reached Chingford, and here the horses were taken out and the drag, on which they were to lunch, drawn up in a sheltered spot. They were all rather hungry, but as it was not yet feeding-time, they scattered to have drinks meanwhile. Liza and Tom, with Sally and her young man, went off together to the nearest public-house, and as they drank beer, Harry, who was a great sportsman, gave them a graphic account of a prize-fight he had seen on the previous Saturday evening, which had been rendered specially memorable by one man being so hurt that he had died from the effects. It had evidently been a very fine affair, and Harry said that several swells from the West End had been present, and he related their ludicrous efforts to get in without being seen by anyone, and their terror when someone to frighten them called out "Copper!" Then Tom and he entered into a discussion on the subject of boxing, in which Tom, being a shy and undogmatic sort of person, was entirely worsted. After this they strolled back to the brake, and found things being prepared for luncheon; the hampers were brought out and emptied, and the bottles of beer in great profusion made many a thirsty mouth thirstier.

"Come along, lidies an' gentlemen—if you are gentlemen," shouted the coachman; "the animals is now goin' ter be fed!"

"Garn awy," answered somebody, "we're not hanimals; we don't drink water."

"You're too clever," remarked the coachman; "I can see you've just come from the board school."

As the former speaker was a lady of quite mature appearance, the remark was not without its little irony. The other man blew his horn by way of grace, at which Liza called out to him:

"Don't do thet, you'll bust, I know you will, an' if you bust you'll quite spoil my dinner!"

Then they all set to. Pork-pies, saveloys, sausages, cold potatoes, hard-boiled eggs, cold bacon, veal, ham, crabs and shrimps, cheese, butter, cold suet-puddings and treacle, gooseberry-tarts, cherry-tarts, butter, bread, more sausages, and yet again pork-pies! They devoured the provisions like ravening beasts, stolidly, silently, earnestly, in large mouthfuls which they shoved down their throats unmasticated. The intelligent foreigner seeing them thus dispose of their food would have understood why England is a great nation. He would have understood why Britons never, never will be slaves. They never stopped except to drink, and then at each gulp they emptied their glass; no heel-taps! And still they ate, and still they drank—but as all things must cease, they stopped at last, and a long sigh of content broke from their two-and-thirty throats.

Then the gathering broke up, and the good folk paired themselves and separated. Harry and his lady strolled off to secluded byways in the forest, so that they might discourse of their loves and digest their dinner. Tom had all the morning been waiting for this happy moment; he had counted on the expansive effect of a full stomach to thaw his Liza's coldness, and he had pictured himself sitting on the grass with his back against the trunk of a spreading chestnut-tree, with his arm round his Liza's waist, and her head resting affectionately on his manly bosom. Liza, too, had foreseen the separation into couples after dinner, and had been racking her brains to find a means of getting out of it.

"I don't want 'im slobberin' abaht me," she said; "it gives me the sick, all this kissin' an' cuddlin'!"

She scarcely knew why she objected to his caresses; but they bored her and made her cross. But luckily the blessed institution of marriage came to her rescue, for Jim and his wife naturally had no particular desire to spend the afternoon together, and Liza, seeing a little embarrassment on their part, proposed that they should go for a walk together in the forest.

Jim agreed at once, and with pleasure, but Tom was dreadfully disappointed. He hadn't the courage to say anything, but he glared at Blakeston. Jim smiled benignly at him, and Tom began to sulk. Then they began a funny walk through the woods. Jim tried to go on with Liza, and Liza was not at all disinclined to this, for she had come to the conclusion that Jim, notwithstanding his "cheek", was not " 'alf a bad sort". But Tom kept walking alongside of them, and as Jim slightly quickened his pace so as to get Liza on in front, Tom quickened his, and Mrs. Blakeston, who didn't want to be left behind, had to break into a little trot to keep up with them. Jim tried also to get Liza all to himself in the conversation, and let Tom see that he was out in the cold, but Tom would break in with cross, sulky remarks, just to make the others uncomfortable. Liza at last got rather vexed with him.

"Strikes me you got aht of bed the wrong way this mornin'," she said to him.

"Yer didn't think thet when yer said you'd come aht with me." He emphasised the "me".

Liza shrugged her shoulders.

"You give me the 'ump," she said. "If yer wants ter mike a fool of yerself, you can go elsewhere an' do it."

"I suppose yer want me ter go awy now," he said angrily.

"I didn't say I did."

"Arright, Liza, I won't stay where I'm not wanted." And

turning on his heel he marched off, striking through the underwood into the midst of the forest.

He felt extremely unhappy as he wandered on, and there was a choky feeling in his throat as he thought of Liza: she was very unkind and ungrateful, and he wished he had never come to Chingford. She might so easily have come for a walk with him instead of going with that beast of a Blakeston; she wouldn't ever do anything for him, and he hated her—but all the same, he was a poor foolish thing in love, and he began to feel that perhaps he had been a little exacting and a little forward to take offence. And then he wished he had never said anything, and he wanted so much to see her and make it up. He made his way back to Chingford, hoping she would not make him wait too long.

Liza was a little surprised when Tom turned and left them.

"Wot 'as 'e got the needle abaht?" she said.

"Why, 'e's jealous," answered Jim, with a laugh.

"Tom jealous?"

"Yus; 'e's jealous of me."

"Well, 'e ain't got no cause ter be jealous of anyone—that e ain't!" said Liza, and continued by telling him all about Tom: how he had wanted to marry her and she wouldn't have him, and how she had only agreed to come to Chingford with him on the understanding that she should preserve her entire freedom. Jim listened sympathetically, but his wife paid no attention; she was doubtless engaged in thought respecting her household or her family.

When they got back to Chingford they saw Tom standing in solitude looking at them. Liza was struck by the woebegone expression on his face; she felt she had been cruel to him, and leaving the Blakestons went up to him.

"I say, Tom," she said, "don't tike on so; I didn't mean it."

He was bursting to apologise for his behaviour.

"Yer know, Tom," she went on, "I'm rather 'asty, an' I'm sorry I said wot I did."

"Oh, Liza, you are good! You ain't cross with me?"

"Me? Na; it's you thet oughter be cross."

"You are a good sort, Liza!"

"You ain't vexed with me?"

"Give me Liza every time; that's wot I say," he answered, as his face lit up. "Come along an' 'ave tea, an' then we'll go for a donkey-ride."

The donkey-ride was a great success. Liza was a little afraid at first, so Tom walked by her side to take care of her, she screamed the moment the beast began to trot, and clutched hold of Tom to save herself from falling, and as he felt her hand on his shoulder, and heard her appealing cry: "Oh, do 'old me! I'm fallin'!" he felt that he had never in his life been so deliciously happy. The whole party joined in, and it was proposed that they should have races; but in the first heat, when the donkeys broke into a canter, Liza fell off into Tom's arms and the donkey scampered on without her.

"I know wot I'll do," she said, when the runaway had been recovered, "I'll ride 'im straddlewyse."

"Garn!" said Sally, "yer can't with petticoats."

"Yus, I can, an' I will too!"

So another donkey was procured, this time with a man's saddle, and putting her foot in the stirrup, she cocked her leg over and took her seat triumphantly. Neither modesty nor bashfulness was to be reckoned among Liza's faults, and in this position she felt quite at ease.

"I'll git along arright now, Tom," she said; "you garn and git yerself a moke, and come an' jine in."

The next race was perfectly uproarious. Liza kicked and beat her donkey with all her might, shrieking and laughing the while, and finally came in winner by a length. After that they felt rather warm and dry, and repaired to the public-house to restore themselves and talk over the excitements of the racecourse.

When they had drunk several pints of beer Liza and Sally, with their respective adorers and the Blakestons, walked round to find other means of amusing themselves; they were arrested by a coconut-shy.

"Oh, let's 'ave a shy!" said Liza, excitedly, at which the unlucky men had to pull out their coppers, while Sally and Liza made ludicrously bad shots at the coconuts.

"It looks so bloomin' easy," said Liza, brushing up her hair, "but I can't 'it the blasted thing. You 'ave a shot, Tom."

He and Harry were equally unskilful, but Jim got three coconuts running, and the proprietors of the show began to look on him with some concern.

"You are a dab at it," said Liza, in admiration.

They tried to induce Mrs. Blakeston to try her luck, but she stoutly refused.

"I don't 'old with such foolishness. It's wiste of money ter me," she said.

"Na then, don't crack on, old tart," remarked her husband, "let's go an' eat the coconuts."

There was one for each couple, and after the ladies had

sucked the juice they divided them and added their respective shares to their dinners and teas. Supper came next. Again they fell to sausage-rolls, boiled eggs, and saveloys, and countless bottles of beer were added to those already drunk.

"I dunno 'ow many bottles of beer I've drunk—I've lost count," said Liza; whereat there was a general laugh.

They still had an hour before the brake was to start back, and it was then the concertinas came in useful. They sat down on the grass, and the concert was begun by Harry, who played a solo; then there was a call for a song, and Jim stood up and sang that ancient ditty, "O dem Golden Kippers, O". There was no shyness in the company, and Liza, almost without being asked, gave another popular comic song. Then there was more concertina playing, and another demand for a song, Liza turned to Tom, who was sitting quietly by her side.

"Give us a song, old cock," she said.

"I can't," he answered. "I'm not a singin' sort." At which Blakeston got up and offered to sing again.

"Tom is rather a soft," said Liza to herself, "not like that cove Blakeston."

They repaired to the public-house to have a few last drinks before the brake started, and when the horn blew to warn them, rather unsteadily, they proceeded to take their places.

Liza, as she scrambled up the steps, said: "Well, I believe I'm boozed."

The coachman had arrived at the melancholy stage of intoxication, and was sitting on his box holding his reins, with his head bent on his chest. He was thinking sadly of the long-lost days of his youth, and wishing he had been a better man.

Liza had no respect for such holy emotions, and she brought

44

down her fist on the crown of his hat, and bashed it over his eyes.

"Na then, old jellybelly," she said, "wot's the good of 'avin' a fice as long as a kite?"

He turned round and smote her.

"Jellybelly yerself!" said he.

"Puddin' fice!" she cried.

"Kite fice!"

"Boss eye!"

She was tremendously excited, laughing and singing, keeping the whole company in an uproar. In her jollity she had changed hats with Tom, and he in her big feathers made her shriek with laughter. When they started they began to sing "For 'e's a jolly good feller", making the night resound with their noisy voices.

Liza and Tom and the Blakestons had got a seat together, Liza being between the two men. Tom was perfectly happy, and only wished that they might go on so for ever. Gradually as they drove along they became quieter, their singing ceased, and they talked in undertones. Some of them slept; Sally and her young man were leaning up against one another, slumbering quite peacefully. The night was beautiful, the sky still blue, very dark, scattered over with countless brilliant stars, and Liza, as she looked up at the heavens, felt a certain emotion, as if she wished to be taken in someone's arms, or feel some strong man's caress; and there was in her heart a strange sensation as though it were growing big. She stopped speaking, and all four were silent. Then slowly she felt Tom's arm steal round her waist, cautiously, as though it were afraid of being there; this time both she and Tom were happy. But suddenly there was a movement on the other side of her, a

4

hand was advanced along her leg, and her hand was grasped and gently pressed. It was Jim Blakeston. She stared a little and began trembling so that Tom noticed it, and whispered:

"You're cold, Liza."

"Na, I'm not, Tom; it's only a sort of shiver thet went through me."

His arm gave her waist a squeeze, and at the same time the big rough hand pressed her little one. And so she sat between them till they reached the "Red Lion" in the Westminster Bridge Road, and Tom said to himself: "I believe she does care for me after all."

When they got down they all said good night, and Sally and Liza, with their respective slaves and the Blakestons, marched off homewards. At the corner of Vere Street Harry said to Tom and Blakeston:

"I say, you blokes, let's go an' 'ave another drink before closin' time."

"I don't mind," said Tom, "after we've took the gals 'ome."

"Then we shan't 'ave time, it's just on closin' time now," answered Harry.

"Well, we can't leave 'em 'ere."

"Yus, you can," said Sally. "No one'll run away with us."

Tom did not want to part from Liza, but she broke in with:

"Yus, go on, Tom. Sally an' me'll git along arright, an' you ain't got too much time."

"Yus, good night, 'Arry," said Sally to settle the matter.

"Good night, old gal," he answered, "give us another slobber."

And she, not at all unwilling, surrendered herself to him, while he imprinted two sounding kisses on her cheeks.

"Good night, Tom," said Liza, holding out her hand.

"Good night, Liza," he answered, taking it, but looking very wistfully at her.

She understood, and with a kindly smile lifted up her face to him. He bent down and, taking her in his arms, kissed her passionately

"You do kiss nice, Liza," he said, making the others laugh.

"Thanks for tikin me aht, old man," she said as they parted.

"Arright, Liza," he answered, and added, almost to himself: "God bless yer!"

" 'Ulloa, Blakeston, ain't you comin'?" said Harry, seeing that Jim was walking off with his wife instead of joining him and Tom.

"Na," he answered, "I'm goin' 'ome. I've got ter be up at five ter-morrer."

"You are a chap!" said Harry, disgustedly, strolling off with Tom to the pub, while the others made their way down the sleeping street.

The house where Sally lived came first, and she left them; then, walking a few yards more, they came to the Blakeston's, and after a little talk at the door Liza bade the couple good night, and was left to walk the rest of the way home. The street was perfectly silent, and the lamp-posts, far apart, threw a dim light which only served to make Liza realise her solitude. There was such a difference between the street at midday, with its swarms of people, and now, when there was neither sound nor soul besides herself, that even she was struck by it. The regular line of houses on either side, with the even pavements and straight, cemented road, seemed to her like some desert place, as if everyone were dead, or a fire had

47

raged and left it all desolate. Suddenly she heard a footstep, she started and looked back. It was a man hurrying behind her, and in a moment she had recognised Jim. He beckoned to her, and in a low voice called:

"Liza!"

She stopped till he had come up to her.

"Wot 'ave yer come aht again for?" she said.

"I've come aht ter say good night to you, Liza," he answered.

"But yer said good night a moment ago."

"I wanted to say it again—properly."

"Where's yer missus?"

"Oh, she's gone in. I said I was dry and was goin' ter 'ave a drink after all."

"But she'll know yer didn't go ter the pub."

"Na, she won't, she's gone straight upstairs to see after the kid. I wanted ter see yer alone, Liza."

"Why?"

He didn't answer, but tried to take hold of her hand. She drew it away quickly. They walked in silence till they came to Liza's house.

"Good night," said Liza.

"Won't you come for a little walk, Liza?"

"Tike care no one 'ears you," she added, in a whisper, though why she whispered she did not know.

"Will yer?" he asked again.

"Na—you've got to get up at five."

"Oh, I only said thet not ter go inter the pub with them."

"So as yer might come 'ere with me?" asked Liza.

"Yus!"

"No, I'm not comin'. Good night."

"Well, say good night nicely."

"Wot d'yer mean?"

"Tom said you did kiss nice."

She looked at him without speaking, and in a moment he had clasped his arms round her, almost lifting her off her feet, and kissed her. She turned her face away.

"Give us yer lips, Liza," he whispered—"give us yer lips."

He turned her face without resistance and kissed her on the mouth.

At last she tore herself from him, and opening the door slid away into the house.

CHAPTER VI

NEXT morning on her way to the factory Liza came up with Sally. They were both of them rather stale and bedraggled after the day's outing; their fringes were ragged and untidily straying over their foreheads, their back hair, carelessly tied in a loose knot, fell over their necks and threatened completely to come down. Liza had not had time to put her hat on, and was holding it in her hand. Sally's was pinned on sideways, and she had to bash it down on her head every now and then to prevent its coming off. Cinderella herself was not more transformed than they were; but Cinderella even in her rags was virtuously tidy and patched up, while Sally had a great tear in her shabby dress, and Liza's stockings were falling over her boots.

"Wot cheer, Sal!" said Liza, when she caught her up.

"Oh, I 'ave got sich a 'ead on me this mornin'!" she remarked, turning round a pale face: heavily lined under the eyes.

"I don't feel too chirpy neither," said Liza, sympathetically.

"I wish I 'adn't drunk so much beer," added Sally, as a pang shot through her head.

"Oh, you'll be arright in a bit," said Liza. Just then they heard the clock strike eight, and they began to run so that they might not miss getting their tokens and thereby their day's pay; they turned into the street at the end of which was the factory, and saw half a hundred women running like themselves to get in before it was too late.

All the morning Liza worked in a dead-and-alive sort of

fashion, her head like a piece of lead with electric shocks going through it when she moved, and her tongue and mouth hot and dry. At last lunch-time came.

"Come on, Sal," said Liza, "I'm goin' to 'ave a glass o' bitter. I can't stand this no longer."

So they entered the public-house opposite, and in one draught finished their pots. Liza gave a long sigh of relief.

"That bucks you up, don't it?"

"I was dry! I ain't told yer yet, Liza, 'ave I? 'E got it aht last night."

"Who d'yer mean?"

"Why, 'Arry. 'E spit it aht at last."

"Arst yer ter nime the day?" said Liza, smiling.

"Thet's it."

"And did yer?"

"Didn't I jest!" answered Sally, with some emphasis. "I always told yer I'd git off before you.'

"Yus! said Liza, thinking.

"Yer know, Liza, you'd better tike Tom; 'e ain't a bad sort." She was quite patronising.

"I'm goin' ter tike 'oo I like; an' it ain't nobody's business but mine."

"Arright, Liza, don't get shirty over it; I don't mean no offence."

"What d'yer say it for then?'

"Well, I thought as seeing as yer'd gone aht with 'im yesterday thet yer meant ter after all."

" 'E wanted ter tike me; I didn't arsk 'im "

"Well, I didn't arsk my 'Arry, either."

"I never said yer did," replied Liza.

"Oh, you've got the 'ump, you 'ave!" finished Sally, rather angrily.

The beer had restored Liza; she went back to work without a headache, and, except for a slight languor, feeling no worse for the previous day's debauch. As she worked on she began going over in her mind the events of the preceding day, and she found entwined in all her thoughts the burly person of Jim Blakeston. She saw him walking by her side in the Forest, presiding over the meals, playing the concertina, singing, joking, and finally, on the drive back, she felt the heavy form by her side, and the big, rough hand holding hers, while Tom's arm was round her waist. Tom! That was the first time he had entered her mind, and he sank into a shadow beside the other. Last of all she remembered the walk home from the pub, the good nights, and the rapid footstep as Jim caught her up, and the kiss. She blushed and looked up quickly to see whether any of the girls were looking at her; she could not help thinking of that moment when he took her in his arms; she still felt the roughness of his beard pressing on her mouth. Her heart seemed to grow larger in her breast, and she caught for breath as she threw back her head as if to receive his lips again. A shudder ran through her from the vividness of the thought.

"Wot are you shiverin' for, Liza?" asked one of the girls. "You ain't cold."

"Not much," answered Liza, blushing awkwardly on her meditations being broken into. "Why, I'm sweatin' so—I'm drippin' wet."

"I expect yer caught cold in the Faurest yesterday."

"I see your mash as I was comin' along this mornin'."

Liza stared a little.

"I ain't got one, 'oo d'yer mean, ay?"

"Yer only Tom, of course. 'E did look washed aht. Wot was yer doin' with 'im yesterday?"

" 'E ain't got nothin' ter do with me, 'e ain't."

"Garn, don't you tell me!"

The bell rang, and, throwing over their work, the girls trooped off, and after chattering in groups outside the factory gates for a while, made their way in different directions to their respective homes. Liza and Sally went along together.

"I sy, we are comin' aht!" cried Sally, seeing the advertisement of a play being acted at the neighbouring theatre.

"I should like ter see thet!" said Liza, as they stood arm-in-arm in front of the flaring poster. It represented two rooms and a passage in between; in one room a dead man was lying on the floor, while two others were standing horror-stricken, listening to a youth who was in the passage, knocking at the door.

"You see, they've killed 'im," said Sally, excitedly.

"Yus, any fool can see thet! an' the one ahtside, wot's 'e doin' of?"

"Ain't 'e beautiful? I'll git my 'Arry ter tike me, I will. I should like ter see it. 'E said 'e'd tike me to the ply."

They strolled on again, and Liza, leaving Sally, made her way to her mother's. She knew she must pass Jim's house, and wondered whether she would see him. But as she walked along the street she saw Tom coming the opposite way, with a sudden impulse she turned back so as not to meet him, and began walking the way she had come. Then thinking herself a fool for what she had done, she turned again and walked towards him. She wondered if he had seen her or noticed her movement, but when she looked down the street he was nowhere to be seen; he had not caught sight of her, and had evidently gone in to see a mate in one or other of the houses. She quickened her step, and passing the house where lived Jim, could not help looking up; he was standing at the door watching her, with a smile on his lips.

"I didn't see yer, Mr Blakeston," she said, as he came up to her.

"Didn't yer? Well, I knew yer would; an' I was witin' for yer ter look up. I see yer before ter-day."

"Na, when?"

"I passed be'ind yer as you an' thet other girl was lookin' at the advertisement of thet ply."

"I never see yer."

"Na, I know yer didn't. I 'ear yer say, you says: 'I should like to see thet.' "

"Yus, an' I should too."

"Well, I'll tike yer."

"You?"

"Yus; why not?"

"I like thet; wot would yer missus sy?"

"She wouldn't know."

"But the neighbours would!"

"No, they wouldn't, no one 'd see us."

He was speaking in a low voice so that people could not hear.

"You could meet me ahtside the theatre," he went on.

"Na, I couldn't go with you; you're a married man."

"Garn! wot's thet matter—jest ter go ter the ply? An'

54

besides, my missus can't come if she wanted, she's got the kids ter look after."

"I should like ter see it," said Liza meditatively.

They had reached her house, and Jim said:

"Well, come aht this evenin' and tell me if yer will—eh, Liza?"

"Na, I'm not comin' aht this evening."

"Thet won't 'urt yer. I shall wite for yer."

" 'Tain't a bit of good your witin', 'cause I shan't come."

"Well, then, look 'ere, Liza; next Saturday night's the last night, an' I shall go to the theatre, any'ow. An' if you'll come, you just come to the door at 'alf-past six, an' you'll find me there. See?"

"Na, I don't," said Liza, firmly.

"Well, I shall expect yer."

"I shan't come, so you needn't expect." And with that she walked into the house and slammed the door behind her.

Her mother had not come in from her day's charing, and Liza set about getting her tea. She thought it would be rather lonely eating it alone, so pouring out a cup of tea and putting a little condensed milk into it, she cut a huge piece of bread-and-butter, and sat herself down outside on the doorstep. Another woman came downstairs, and seeing Liza, sat down by her side and began to talk.

"Why, Mrs. Stanley, wot 'ave yer done to your 'ead?" asked Liza, noticing a bandage round her forehead.

"I 'ad an accident last night," answered the woman, blushing uneasily.

"Oh, I am sorry! Wot did yer do to yerself?"

"I fell against the coal-scuttle and cut my 'ead open."

"Well, I never!"

"To tell yer the truth, I 'ad a few words with my old man. But one doesn't like them things to get abaht; yer won't tell anyone, will yer?"

"Not me!" answered Liza. "I didn't know yer husband was like thet."

"Oh, 'e's as gentle as a lamb when 'e's sober," said Mrs. Stanley, apologetically. "But, Lor' bless yer, when 'e's 'ad a drop too much 'e's a demond, an' there's no two ways abaht it."

"An' you ain't been married long, neither?" said Liza.

"Na, not above eighteen months; ain't it disgriceful? Thet's wot the doctor at the 'orspital says ter me. I 'ad ter go ter the 'orspital. You should have seen 'ow it bled!—it bled all dahn' my fice, and went streamin' like a bust water-pipe. Well, it fair frightened my old man, an' I says ter 'im, 'I'll charge yer,' an' although I was bleedin' like a bloomin' pig I shook my fist at 'im, an' I says, 'I'll charge ye—see if I don't!' An' 'e says, 'Na,' says 'e, 'don't do thet, for God's sike, Kitie, I'll git three months.' 'An' serve yer damn well right!' says I, an' I went aht an' left 'im. But, Lor' bless yer, I wouldn't charge 'im! I know 'e don't mean it; 'e's as gentle as a lamb when 'e's sober." She smiled quite affectionately as she said this.

"Wot did yer do, then?" asked Liza.

"Well, as I wos tellin' yer, I went to the 'orspital, an' the doctor 'e says to me, 'My good woman,' says 'e, 'you might have been very seriously injured.' An' me not been married eighteen months! An' as I was tellin' the doctor all about it, 'Missus,' 'e says ter me, lookin' at me straight in the eyeball, 'Missus,' says 'e, ' 'ave you been drinkin'?' 'Drinkin'?' says I;

'no! I've 'ad a little drop, but as for drinkin'! 'Mind,' says I, 'I don't say I'm a teetotaller—I'm not, I 'ave my glass of beer, and I like it. I couldn't do withaht it, wot with the work I 'ave, I must 'ave somethin' ter keep me tergether. But as for drinkin' 'eavily! Well, I can say this, there ain't a soberer woman than myself in all London. Why, my first 'usband never touched a drop. Ah, my fust 'usband, 'e was a beauty, 'e was.'"

She stopped the repetition of her conversation and addressed herself to Liza.

" 'E was thet different ter this one. 'E was a man as 'ad seen better days. 'E was a gentleman!" She mouthed the word and emphasised it with an expressive nod.

" 'E was a gentleman and a Christian. 'E'd been in good circumstances in 'is time; an' 'e was a man of education and a teetotaller, for twenty-two years."

At that moment Liza's mother appeared on the scene.

"Good evenin', Mrs. Stanley," she said, politely.

"The sime ter you, Mrs. Kemp," replied that lady, with equal courtesy.

"An' 'ow is your poor 'ead?" asked Liza's mother, with sympathy.

"Oh, it's been achin' cruel. I've hardly known wot ter do with myself."

"I'm sure 'e ought ter be ashimed of 'imself for treatin' yer like thet."

"Oh, it wasn't 'is blows I minded so much, Mrs. Kemp," replied Mrs. Stanley, "an' don't you think it. It was wot 'e said ter me. I can stand a blow as well as any woman. I don't mind thet, an' when 'e don't tike a mean advantage of me I can stand up for myself an' give as good as I tike; an' many's the time I give my fust husband a black eye. But the language 'e used, an' the things 'e called me! It made me blush to the roots of my 'air; I'm not used ter bein' spoken ter like thet. I was in good circumstances when my fust 'usband was alive, 'e earned between two an' three pound a week, 'e did. As I said to 'im this mornin', ' 'Ow a gentleman can use sich language, I dunno.' "

" 'Usbands is cautions, 'owever good they are," said Mrs. Kemp, aphoristically. "But I mustn't stay aht 'ere in the night air."

" 'As yer rheumatism been troublin' yer litely?" asked Mrs. Stanley.

"Oh, cruel. Liza rubs me with embrocation every night, but it torments me cruel."

Mrs. Kemp then went into the house, and Liza remained talking to Mrs. Stanley, she, too, had to go in, and Liza was left alone. Some while she spent thinking of nothing, staring vacantly in front of her, enjoying the cool and quiet of the evening. But Liza could not be left alone long, several boys came along with a bat and a ball, and fixed upon the road just in front of her for their pitch. Taking off their coats they piled them up at the two ends, and were ready to begin.

"I say, old gal," said one of them to Liza, "come an' have a gime of cricket, will yer?"

"Na, Bob, I'm tired."

"Come on!"

"Na, I tell you I won't."

"She was on the booze yesterday, an' she ain't got over it," cried another boy.

"I'll swipe yer over the snitch!" replied Liza to him, and then on being asked again, said:

"Leave me alone, won't yer?"

"Liza's got the needle ter-night, thet's flat," commented a third member of the team.

"I wouldn't drink if I was you, Liza," added another, with mock gravity. "It's a bad 'abit ter git into," and he began rolling and swaying about like a drunken man.

If Liza had been "in form" she would have gone straight away and given the whole lot of them a sample of her strength; but she was only rather bored and vexed that they should disturb her quietness, so she let them talk. They saw she was not to be drawn, and leaving her, set to their game. She watched them for some time, but her thoughts gradually lost themselves, and insensibly her mind was filled with a burly form, and she was again thinking of Jim.

" 'E is a good sort ter want ter tike me ter the ply," she said to herself. "Tom never arst me!"

Jim had said he would come out in the evening; he ought to be here soon, she thought. Of course she wasn't going to the theatre with him, but she didn't mind talking to him; she rather enjoyed being asked to do a thing and refusing, and she would have liked another opportunity of doing so. But he didn't come, and he had said he would!

"I say, Bill," she said at last to one of the boys who was fielding close beside her, "that there Blakeston—d'you know 'im?"

"Yes, rather; why, he works at the sime plice as me."

"Wot's 'e do with 'isself in the evening; I never see 'im abaht?"

"I dunno. I see 'im this evenin' go into the 'Red Lion'. I suppose 'e's there, but I dunno."

Then he wasn't coming. Of course she had told him she was going to stay indoors, but he might have come all the same—just to see.

"I know Tom 'ud 'ave come," she said to herself, rather sulkily.

"Liza! Liza!" she heard her mother's voice calling her.

"Arright, I'm comin'," said Liza.

"I've been witin' for you this last 'alf-hour ter rub me."

"Why didn't yer call?" asked Liza.

"I did call. I've been callin' this last I dunno 'ow long; it's give me quite a sore throat."

"I never 'eard yer."

"Na, yer didn't want ter 'ear me, did yer? Yer don't mind if I dies with rheumatics, do yer? I know."

Liza did not answer, but took the bottle, and, pouring some of the liniment on her hand, began to rub it into Mrs. Kemp's rheumatic joints, while the invalid kept complaining and grumbling at everything Liza did.

"Don't rub so 'ard, Liza, you'll rub all the skin off."

Then when Liza did it as gently as she could, she grumbled again.

"If you do it like thet, it won't do no good at all. You want ter sive yerself trouble—I know yer. When I was young girls didn't mind a little bit of 'ard work—but, law bless yer, you don't care abaht my rheumatics, do yer?"

At last she finished, and Liza went to bed by her mother's side.

CHAPTER VII

TWO days passed, and it was Friday morning. Liza had got up early and strolled off to her work in good time, but she did not meet her faithful Sally on the way, nor find her at the factory when she herself arrived. The bell rang and all the girls trooped in, but still Sally did not come. Liza could not make it out, and was thinking she would be shut out, when just as the man who gave out the tokens for the day's work was pulling down the shutter in front of his window, Sally arrived, breathless and perspiring.

"Whew! Go' lumme, I am 'ot!" she said, wiping her face with her apron.

"I thought you wasn't comin'," said Liza.

"Well, I only just did it; I overslep' myself. I was aht lite last night."

"Were yer?"

"Me an' 'Arry went ter see the ply. Oh, Liza, it's simply spiffin'! I've never see sich a good ply in my life. Lor'! Why, it mikes yer blood run cold: they 'ang a man on the stige; oh, it mide me creep all over!"

And then she began telling Liza all about it—the blood and thunder, the shooting, the railway train, the murder, the bomb, the hero, the funny man—jumbling everything up in her excitement, repeating little scraps of dialogue—all wrong —gesticulating, getting excited and red in the face at the recollection. Liza listened rather crossly, feeling bored at the detail into which Sally was going; the piece really didn't much interest her.

5

"One 'ud think yer'd never been to a theatre in your life before," she said.

"I never seen anything so good, I can tell yer. You tike my tip, and git Tom ter tike yer."

"I don't want ter go; an' if I did I'd py for myself an' go alone."

"Cheese it! That ain't 'alf so good. Me an' 'Arry, we set together, 'im with 'is arm round my wiste and me 'oldin' 'is 'and. It was jam, I can tell yer!"

"Well, I don't want anyone sprawlin' me abaht, thet ain't my mark!"

"But I do like 'Arry; you dunno the little ways 'e 'as; an' we're goin' ter be married in three weeks now. 'Arry said, well, 'e says, 'I'll git a licence.' 'Na,' says I, ' 'ave the banns read aht in church; it seems more reg'lar like to 'ave banns; so they're goin' ter be read aht next Sunday. You'll come with me an' 'ear them, won't yer, Liza?"

"Yus, I don't mind."

On the way home Sally insisted on stopping in front of the poster and explaining to Liza all about the scene represented.

"Oh, you give me the sick with your 'Fital Card', you do! I'm goin' 'ome." And she left Sally in the midst of her explanation.

"I dunno wot's up with Liza," remarked Sally to a mutual friend. "She's always got the needle, some-'ow."

"Oh, she's barmy," answered the friend.

"Well, I do think she's a bit dotty sometimes—I do really," rejoined Sally.

Liza walked homewards, thinking of the play; at length she tossed her head impatiently.

"I don't want ter see the blasted thing; an' if I see that there Jim I'll tell 'im so; swop me bob, I will."

She did see him; he was leaning with his back against the wall of his house, smoking. Liza knew he had seen her, and as she walked by pretended not to have noticed him. To her disgust, he let her pass, and she was thinking he hadn't seen her after all, when she heard him call her name.

"Liza!"

She turned round and started with surprise very well imitated. "I didn't see you was there!" she said.

"Why did yer pretend not ter notice me, as yer went past—eh, Liza?"

"Why, I didn't see yer."

"Garn! But you ain't shirty with me?"

"Wot 'ave I got to be shirty abaht?"

He tried to take her hand, but she drew it away quickly. She was getting used to the movement. They went on talking, but Jim did not mention the theatre; Liza was surprised, and wondered whether he had forgotten.

"Er—Sally went to the ply last night," she said, at last.

"Oh!" he said, and that was all.

She got impatient.

"Well, I'm off!" she said.

"Na, don't go yet; I want ter talk ter yer," he replied.

"Wot abaht? anythin' in partickler?" She would drag it out of him if she possibly could.

"Not thet I knows on," he said, smiling.

"Good night!" she said, abruptly, turning away from him.

"Well, I'm damned if 'e ain't forgotten!" she said to herself, sulkily, as she marched home.

The following evening about six o'clock, it suddenly struck her that it was the last night of the "New and Sensational Drama".

"I do like thet Jim Blakeston," she said to herself; "fancy treatin' me like thet! You wouldn't catch Tom doin' sich a thing. Bli'me if I speak to 'im again, the—— Now I shan't see it at all. I've a good mind ter go on my own 'ook. Fancy 'is forgettin' all abaht it, like thet!"

She was really quite indignant; though, as she had distinctly refused Jim's offer, it was rather hard to see why.

" 'E said 'e'd wite for me ahtside the doors; I wonder if 'e's there. I'll go an' see if 'e is, see if I don't—an' then if 'e's there, I'll go in on my own'ook, jist ter spite 'im!"

She dressed herself in her best, and, so that the neighbours shouldn't see her, went up a passage between some model lodging-house buildings, and in this roundabout way got into the Westminster Bridge Road, and soon found herself in front of the theatre.

"I've been witin' for yer this 'alf-hour."

She turned round and saw Jim standing just behind her.

" 'Oo are you talkin' to? I'm not goin' to the ply with you. Wot d'yer tike me for, eh?"

" 'Oo are yer goin' with, then?"

"I'm goin' alone."

"Garn! don't be a bloomin' jackass!"

Liza was feeling very injured.

"Thet's 'ow you treat me! I shall go 'ome. Why didn't you come aht the other night?"

"Yer told me not ter."

She snorted at the ridiculous ineptitude of the reply.

"Why didn't you say nothin' abaht it yesterday?"

"Why, I thought you'd come if I didn't talk on it."

"Well, I think you're a——brute!" She felt very much nclined to cry.

"Come on, Liza, don't tike on; I didn't mean no offence." And he put his arm round her waist and led her to take their places at the gallery door. Two tears escaped from the corners of her eyes and ran down her nose, but she felt very relieved and happy, and let him lead her where he would.

There was a long string of people waiting at the door, and Liza was delighted to see a couple of niggers who were helping them to while away the time of waiting. The niggers sang and danced, and made faces, while the people looked on with appreciative gravity, like royalty listening to de Reszké, and they were very generous of applause and halfpence at the end of the performance. Then, when the niggers moved to the pit doors, paper boys came along offering *Tit-Bits* and "extra specials"; after that three little girls came round and sang sentimental songs and collected more halfpence. At last a movement ran through the serpent-like string of people, sounds were heard behind the door, everyone closed up, the men told the women to keep close and hold tight; there was a great unbarring and unbolting, the doors were thrown open, and, like a bursting river, the people surged in.

Half an hour more and the curtain went up. The play was indeed thrilling. Liza quite forgot her companion, and was intent on the scene; she watched the incidents breathlessly, trembling with excitement, almost beside herself at the celebrated hanging incident. When the curtain fell on the first act she sighed and mopped her face.

"See 'ow 'ot I am," she said to Jim, giving him her hand.

"Yus, you are!" he remarked, taking it.

"Leave go!" she said, trying to withdraw it from him.

"Not much," he answered, quite boldly.

"Garn! Leave go!" But he didn't, and she really did not struggle very violently.

The second act came, and she shrieked over the comic man; and her laughter rang higher than anyone else's, so that people turned to look at her, and said:

"She is enjoyin' 'erself."

Then when the murder came she bit her nails and the sweat stood on her forehead in great drops; in her excitement she even called out as loud as she could to the victim, "Look aht!" It caused a laugh and slackened the tension, for the whole house was holding its breath as it looked at the villains listening at the door, creeping silently forward, crawling like tigers to their prey.

Liza trembling all over, and in her terror threw herself against Jim, who put both his arms round her, and said:

"Don't be afride, Liza; it's all right."

At last the men sprang, there was a scuffle, and the wretch was killed, then came the scene depicted on the posters—the victim's son knocking at the door, on the inside of which were the murderers and the murdered man. At last the curtain came down, and the house in relief burst forth into cheers and cheers; the handsome hero in his top hat was greeted thunderously; the murdered man, with his clothes still all disarranged, was hailed with sympathy; and the villains—the house yelled and hissed and booed, while the poor brutes bowed and tried to look as if they liked it.

"I am enjoyin' myself," said Liza, pressing herself quite close to Jim; "you are a good sort ter tike me—Jim."

He gave her a little hug, and it struck her that she was sitting just as Sally had done, and, like Sally, she found it "jam".

The *entr'actes* were short and the curtain was soon up again, and the comic man raised customary laughter by undressing and exposing his nether garments to the public view; then more tragedy, and the final act with its darkened room, its casting lots, and its explosion.

When it was all over and they had got outside Jim smacked his lips and said:

"I could do with a gargle; let's go into thet pub there."

"I'm as dry as bone," said Liza; and so they went.

When they got in they discovered they were hungry, and seeing some appetising sausage-rolls, ate of them, and washed them down with a couple of pots of beer; then Jim lit his pipe and they strolled off. They had got quite near the Westminster Bridge Road when Jim suggested that they should go and have one more drink before closing time.

"I shall be tight," said Liza.

"Thet don't matter," answered Jim, laughing. "You ain't got ter go ter work in the mornin' an' you can sleep it aht."

"Arright, I don't mind if I do then, in for a penny, in for a pound."

At the pub door she drew back.

"I say, guv'ner," she said, "there'll be some of the coves from dahn our street, and they'll see us."

"Na, there won't be nobody there, don't yer 'ave no fear."

"I don't like ter go in for fear of it."

"Well, we ain't doin' no 'arm if they does see us, an' we can go into the private bar, an' you bet your boots there won't be no one there."

She yielded, and they went in.

"Two pints of bitter, please, miss," ordered Jim.

"I say, 'old 'ard. I can't drink more than 'alf a pint," said Liza.

"Cheese it," answered Jim. "You can do with all you can get, I know."

At closing time they left and walked down the broad road which led homewards.

"Let's 'ave a little sit dahn," said Jim, pointing to an empty bench between two trees.

"Na, it's gettin' lite; I want ter be 'ome."

"It's such a fine night, it's a pity ter go in already;" and he drew her unresisting towards the seat. He put his arm round her waist.

"Un'and me, villin!" she said, in apt misquotation of the melodrama, but Jim only laughed, and she made no effort to disengage herself.

They sat there for a long while in silence; the beer had got to Liza's head, and the warm night air filled her with a double intoxication. She felt the arm round her waist, and the big, heavy form pressing against her side; she experienced again the curious sensation as if her heart were about to burst, and it choked her—a feeling so oppressive and painful that it almost made her feel sick. Her hands began to tremble, and her breathing grew rapid, as though she were suffocating. Almost fainting, she swayed over towards the man, and a cold shiver ran through her from top to toe. Jim bent over her, and,

68

taking her in both arms, he pressed his lips to hers in a long, passionate kiss. At last, panting for breath, she turned her head away and groaned.

Then they again sat for a long while in silence, Liza full of a strange happiness, feeling as if she could laugh aloud hysterically, but restrained by the calm and silence of the night. Close behind struck a church clock—one.

"Bless my soul!" said Liza, starting, "there's one o'clock I must get 'ome."

"It's so nice out 'ere; do sty, Liza." He pressed her closer to him. "Yer know, Liza, I love yer—fit ter kill."

"Na, I can't stay; come on." She got up from the seat, and pulled him up too. "Come on," she said.

Without speaking they went along, and there was no one to be seen either in front or behind them. He had not got his arm round her now, and they were walking side by side, slightly separated. It was Liza who spoke first.

"You'd better go dahn the Road and by the church an' git into Vere Street the other end, an' I'll go through the passage, so thet no one shouldn't see us comin' together," she spoke almost in a whisper.

"Arright, Liza," he answered, "I'll do just as you tell me."

They came to the passage of which Liza spoke; it was a narrow way between blank walls, the backs of factories, and it led into the upper end of Vere Street. The entrance to it was guarded by two iron posts in the middle, so that horses or barrows should not be taken through.

They had just got to it when a man came out into the open road. Liza quickly turned her head away.

"I wonder if 'e see us," she said, when he had passed out of earshot. " 'E's lookin' back," she added.

"Why, 'oo is it?" asked Jim.

"It's a man aht of our street," she answered. "I dunno 'im, but I know where 'e lodges. D'yer think 'e see us?"

"Na, 'e wouldn't know 'oo it was in the dark."

"But he looked round; all the street'll know it if he see us."

"Well, we ain't doin' no 'arm."

She stetched out her hand to say good night.

"I'll come a little wy with yer along the passage," said Jim.

"Na, you mustn't; you go straight round."

"But it's so dark; p'raps summat'll 'appen to yer."

"Not it! You go on 'ome an' leave me," she replied, and entering the passage, stood facing him with one of the iron pillars between them.

"Good night, old cock," she said, stretching out her hand. He took it, and said:

"I wish yer wasn't goin' ter leave me, Liza."

"Garn! I must!" She tried to get her hand away from his, but he held it firm, resting it on the top of the pillar.

"Leave go my 'and," she said. He made no movement, but looked into her eyes steadily, so that it made her uneasy. She repented having come out with him. "Leave go my 'and." And she beat down on his with her closed fist.

"Liza!" he said, at last.

"Well, wot is it?" she answered, still thumping down on his hand with her fist.

"Liza," he said in a whisper, "will yer?"

"Will I wot?" she said, looking down.

"You know, Liza. Sy, will yer?"

"Na," she said.

He bent over her and repeated—

"Will yer?"

She did not speak, but kept beating down on his hand.

"Liza," he said again, his voice growing hoarse and thick—
"Liza, will yer?"

She still kept silence, looking away and continually bringing
down her fist. He looked at her a moment, and she, ceasing to
thump his hand, looked up at him with half-opened mouth.
Suddenly he shook himself, and closing his fist gave her a
violent, swinging blow in the belly.

"Come on," he said.

And together they slid down into the darkness of the
passage.

CHAPTER VIII

MRS. KEMP was in the habit of slumbering somewhat heavily on Sunday mornings, or Liza would not have been allowed to go on sleeping as she did. When she woke, she rubbed her eyes to gather her senses together and gradually she remembered having gone to the theatre on the previous evening; then suddenly everything came back to her. She stretched out her legs and gave a long sigh of delight. Her heart was full; she thought of Jim, and the delicious sensation of love came over her. Closing her eyes, she imagined his warm kisses, and she lifted up her arms as if to put them round his neck and draw him down to her; she almost felt the rough beard on her face, and the strong heavy arms round her body. She smiled to herself and took a long breath; then, slipping back the sleeves of her nightdress, she looked at her own thin arms, just two pieces of bone with not a muscle on them, but very white and showing distinctly the interlacement of blue veins; she did not notice that her hands were rough, and red and dirty with the nails broken, and bitten to the quick. She got out of bed and looked at herself in the glass over the mantelpiece; with one hand she brushed back her hair and smiled at herself; her face was very small and thin, but the complexion was nice, clear and white, with a delicate tint of red on the cheeks, and her eyes were big and dark like her hair She felt very happy.

She did not want to dress yet, but rather to sit down and think, so she twisted up her hair into a little knot, slipped a skirt over her nightdress, and sat on a chair near the window and began looking around. The decorations of the room had been centred on the mantelpiece; the chief ornament consisted of a pear and an apple, a pineapple, a bunch of grapes, and several fat plums, all very beautifully done in wax, as was the fashion about the middle of this most glorious reign. They were appropriately coloured—the apple blushing red, the grapes an inky black, emerald green leaves were scattered here and there to lend finish, and the whole was mounted on an ebonised stand covered with black velvet, and protected from dust and dirt by a beautiful glass cover bordered with red plush. Liza's eyes rested on this with approbation, and the pineapple quite made her mouth water. At either end of the mantelpiece were pink jars with blue flowers on the front; round the top in Gothic letters of gold was inscribed: "A Present from a Friend"—these were products of a later, but not less artistic age. The intervening spaces were taken up with little jars and cups and saucers—gold inside, with a view of a town outside, and surrounding them, "A Present from Clacton-on-Sea," or, alliteratively, "A Memento of Margate." Of these many were broken, but they had been mended with glue, and it is well known that pottery in the eyes of the connoisseur loses none of its value by a crack or two. Then there were portraits innumerable—little yellow cartes-de-visite in velvet frames, some of which were decorated with shells; they showed strange people with old-fashioned clothes, the women with bodices and sleeves fitting close to the figure, stern-featured females with hair carefully parted in the middle and plastered down on each side, firm chins and mouths, with small, pig-like eyes and wrinkled faces, and the men were uncomfortably clad in Sunday garments, very stiff and uneasy in their awkward postures, with large whiskers and shaved chins and upper lips and a general air of horny-handed toil. Then there were one or two daguerreotypes, little full-length figures framed in gold paper. There was one of Mrs. Kemp's father and one of her mother, and there were several photographs of betrothed or newly-married couples, the lady sitting down and the man standing behind her with his hand on the chair, or the man sitting and the woman with her hand on his shoulder. And from all sides of the room, standing on the mantelpiece, hanging above it, on the wall and over the bed, they stared full-face into the room, self-consciously fixed for ever in their stiff discomfort.

The walls were covered with dingy, antiquated paper, and ornamented with coloured supplements from Christmas Numbers—there was a very patriotic picture of a soldier shaking the hand of a fallen comrade and waving his arm in defiance of a band of advancing Arabs; there was a "Cherry Ripe," almost black with age and dirt; there were two almanacks several years old, one with a coloured portrait of the Marquess of Lorne, very handsome and elegantly dressed, the object of Mrs. Kemp's adoration since her husband's demise; the other a Jubilee portrait of the Queen, somewhat losing in dignity by a moustache which Liza in an irreverent moment had smeared on with charcoal.

The furniture consisted of a wash-hand stand and a little deal chest of drawers, which acted as sideboard to such pots and and pans and crockery as could not find room in the grate; and besides the bed there was nothing but two kitchen chairs and a lamp. Liza looked at it all and felt perfectly satisfied; she put a pin into one corner of the noble Marquess to prevent him from falling, fiddled about with the ornaments a little, and then started washing herself. After putting on her clothes she ate some bread-and-butter, swallowed a dishful of cold tea, and went out into the street.

She saw some boys playing cricket and went up to them.

"Let me ply," she said.

"Arright, Liza," cried half a dozen of them in delight; and the captain added: "You go an' scout over by the lamp-post.'

"Go an' scout my eye!" said Liza, indignantly. "When I ply cricket I does the battin'."

"Na, you're not goin' ter bat all the time. 'Oo are you gettin' at?" replied the captain, who had taken advantage of his position to put himself in first, and was still at the wicket.

"Well, then I shan't ply," answered Liza.

"Garn, Ernie, let 'er go in!" shouted two or three members of the team.

"Well, I'm busted!" remarked the captain, as she took his bat. "You won't sty in long, I lay," he said, as he sent the old bowler fielding and took the ball himself. He was a young gentleman who did not suffer from excessive backwardness.

"Aht!" shouted a dozen voices as the ball went past Liza's bat and landed in the pile of coats which formed the wicket. The captain came forward to resume his innings, but Liza held the bat away from him.

"Garn!" she said; "thet was only a trial."

"You never said trial," answered the captain indignantly.

"Yus, I did," said Liza; "I said it just as the ball was comin' —under my breath."

"Well, I am busted!" repeated the captain.

Just then Liza saw Tom among the lookers-on, and as she

felt very kindly disposed to the world in general that morning, she called out to him:

" 'Ulloa, Tom!" she said. "Come an' give us a ball; this chap can't bowl."

"Well, I got yer aht, any'ow," said that person.

"Ah, yer wouldn't 'ave got me aht plyin square. But a trial ball—well, one don't ever know wot a trial ball's goin' ter do."

Tom began bowling very slowly and easily, so that Liza could swing her bat round and hit mightily; she ran well, too, and pantingly brought up her score to twenty. Then the fielders interposed.

"I sy, look 'ere, 'e's only givin' 'er lobs; 'e's not tryin' ter git 'er aht."

"You're spoilin' our gime."

"I don't care; I've got twenty runs—thet's more than you could do. I'll go aht now of my own accord, so there! Come on, Tom."

Tom joined her, and as the captain at last resumed his bat and the game went on, they commenced talking, Liza leaning against the wall of a house, while Tom stood in front of her, smiling with pleasure

"Where 'ave you been 'idin' yerself, Tom? I ain't seen yer for I dunno 'ow long."

"I've been abaht as usual; an' I've seen you when you didn't see me."

"Well, yer might 'ave come up and said good mornin' when you see me."

"I didn't want ter force myself on yer, Liza."

"Garn! You are a bloomin' cuckoo, I'm blowed!"

"I thought yer didn't like me 'angin' round yer; so I kep' awy."

"Why, yer talks as if I didn't like yer. Yer don't think I'd 'ave come aht beanfeastin' with yer if I 'adn't liked yer?"

Liza was really very dishonest, but she felt so happy this morning that she loved the whole world, and of course Tom came in with the others. She looked very kindly at him, and he was so affected that a great lump came in his throat and he could not speak.

Liza's eyes turned to Jim's house, and she saw coming out of the door a girl of about her own age; she fancied she saw in her some likeness to Jim.

"Say, Tom," she asked, "thet ain't Blakeston's daughter, is it?"

"Yus, thet's it."

"I'll go an' speak to 'er," said Liza, leaving Tom and going over the road.

"You're Polly Blakeston, ain't yer?" she said.

"Thet's me!" said the girl.

"I thought you was. Your dad, 'e says ter me, 'You dunno my daughter, Polly, do yer?' says 'e. 'Na,' says I, 'I don't.' Well,' says 'e, 'You can't miss 'er when you see 'er.' An' right enough I didn't."

"Mother says I'm all father, an' there ain't nothin' of 'er in me. Dad says it's lucky it ain't the other wy abaht, or 'e'd 'ave got a divorce."

They both laughed.

"Where are you goin' now?" asked Liza, looking at the slop-basin she was carrying.

6

"I was just goin' dahn into the road ter get some ice-cream for dinner. Father 'ad a bit of luck last night, 'e says, and 'e'd stand the lot of us ice-cream for dinner ter-day."

"I'll come with yer if yer like."

"Come on!" And, already friends, they walked arm-in-arm to the Westminster Bridge Road. Then they went along till they came to a stall where an Italian was selling the required commodity, and having had a taste apiece to see if they liked it, Polly planked down sixpence and had her basin filled with a poisonous-looking mixture of red and white ice-cream.

On the way back, looking up the street, Polly cried:

"There's father!"

Liza's heart beat rapidly and she turned red; but suddenly a sense of shame came over her, and casting down her head so that she might not see him, she said:

"I think I'll be off 'ome an' see 'ow mother's gettin' on." And before Polly could say anything she had slipped away and entered her own house.

Mother was not getting on at all well.

"You've come in at last, you ——, you!" snarled Mrs. Kemp, as Liza entered the room.

"Wot's the matter, mother?"

"Matter! I like thet—matter indeed! Go an' matter yerself an' be mattered! Nice way ter treat an old woman like me— an' yer own mother, too!"

"Wot's up now?"

"Don't talk ter me; I don't want ter listen ter you. Leavin' me all alone, me with my rheumatics, an' the neuralgy! I've 'ad the neuralgy all the mornin', and my 'ead's been simply splittin', so thet I thought the bones 'ud come apart

78

and all my brains go streamin' on the floor. An' when I wake up there's no one ter git my tea for me, an' I lay there witin' an' witin', an' at last I 'ad ter git up and mike it myself. And, my 'ead simply cruel! Why, I might 'ave been burnt ter death with the fire alight an' me asleep."

"Well, I am sorry, mother; but I went aht just for a bit, an' didn't think you'd wike. An' besides, the fire wasn't alight."

"Garn with yer! I didn't treat my mother like thet. Oh, you've been a bad daughter ter me—an' I 'ad more illness carryin' you than with all the other children put togither. You was a cross at yer birth, an' you've been a cross ever since. An' now in my old age, when I've worked myself ter the bone, yer leaves me to starve and burn to death." Here she began to cry, and the rest of her utterances was lost in sobs.

The dusk had darkened into night, and Mrs. Kemp had retired to rest with the dicky-birds. Liza was thinking of many things; she wondered why she had been unwilling to meet Jim in the morning.

"I was a bally fool," she said to herself.

It really seemed an age since the previous night, and all that had happened seemed very long ago. She had not spoken to Jim all day, and she had so much to say to him. Then, wondering whether he was about, she went to the window and looked out; but there was nobody there. She closed the window again and sat just beside it; the time went on, and she wondered whether he would come, asking herself whether he had been thinking of her as she of him; gradually her thoughts grew vague, and a kind of mist came over them. She nodded. Suddenly she roused herself with a start, fancying she had heard something; she listened again, and in a moment the sound was repeated, three or four gentle taps on the window. She opened it quickly and whispered:

"Jim."

"Thet's me,' he answered, "come aht."

Closing the window, she went into the passage and opened the street door; it was hardly unlocked before Jim had pushed his way in; partly shutting it behind him, he took her in his arms and hugged her to his breast. She kissed him passionately.

"I thought yer'd come ter-night, Jim; summat in my 'eart told me so. But you 'ave been long."

"I wouldn't come before, 'cause I thought there'd be people abaht. Kiss us!" And again he pressed his lips to hers, and Liza nearly fainted with the delight of it.

"Let's go for a walk, shall we?" he said.

"Arright!" They were speaking in whispers. "You go into the road through the passage, an' I'll go by the street."

"Yus, thet's right," and kissing her once more, he slid out, and she closed the door behind him.

Then going back to get her hat, she came again into the passage, waiting behind the door till it might be safe for her to venture. She had not made up her mind to risk it, when she heard a key put in the lock, and she hardly had time to spring back to prevent herself from being hit by the opening door. It was a man, one of the upstairs lodgers.

" 'Ulloa!" he said, " 'oo's there?"

"Mr. 'Odges! Strike me, you did give me a turn; I was just goin' aht." She blushed to her hair, but in the darkness he could see nothing.

"Good night," she said, and went out.

She walked close along the sides of the houses like a thief, and the policeman as she passed him turned round and looked at her, wondering whether she was meditating some illegal deed. She breathed freely on coming into the open road, and seeing Jim skulking behind a tree, ran up to him, and in the shadows they kissed again.

CHAPTER IX

THUS began a time of love and joy. As soon as her work was over and she had finished tea, Liza would slip out and at some appointed spot meet Jim. Usually it would be at the church, where the Westminster Bridge Road bends down to get to the river, and they would go off, arm-in-arm, till they came to some place where they could sit down and rest. Sometimes they would walk along the Albert Embankment to Battersea Park, and here sit on the benches, watching the children play. The female cyclist had almost abandoned Battersea for the parks on the other side of the river, but often enough one went by, and Liza, with the old-fashioned prejudice of her class, would look after the rider and make some remark about her, not seldom more forcible than ladylike. Both Jim and she liked children, and tiny, ragged urchins would gather round to have rides on the man's knees or mock fights with Liza.

They thought themselves far away from anyone in Vere Street, but twice, as they were walking along, they were met by people they knew. Once it was two workmen coming home from a job at Vauxhall: Liza did not see them till they were quite near; she immediately dropped Jim's arm, and they both cast their eyes to the ground as the men passed, like ostriches, expecting that if they did not look they would not be seen.

"D'you see 'em, Jim?" asked Liza, in a whisper, when they had gone by. "I wonder if they see us." Almost instinctively she turned round, and at the same moment one of the men turned too; then there was no doubt about it.

"Thet did give me a turn," she said.

"So it did me," answered Jim; "I simply went 'ot all over."

"We was bally fools," said Liza; "we oughter 'ave spoken to 'em! D'you think they'll let aht?"

They heard nothing of it, when Jim afterwards met one of the men in a public-house he did not mention a meeting, and they thought that perhaps they had not been recognised. But the second time was worse.

It was on the Albert Embankment again. They were met by a party of four, all of whom lived in the street. Liza's heart sank within her, for there was no chance of escape; she thought of turning quickly and walking in the opposite direction, but there was not time, for the men had already seen them. She whispered to Jim:

"Back us up," as and they met she said to one of the men:
" 'Ulloa there! Where are you off to?"

The men stopped, and one of them asked the question back.

"Where are you off to?"

"Me? Oh, I've just been to the 'orspital. One of the gals at our place is queer, an' so I says ter myself, 'I'll go an' see 'er.' "
She faltered a little as she began, but quickly gathered herself together, lying fluently and without hesitation.

"An' when I come aht," she went on, " 'oo should I see just passin' the 'orspital but this 'ere cove, an' 'e says to me, 'Wot cheer,' says 'e, 'I'm goin' ter Vaux'all, come an' walk a bit of the wy with us.' 'Arright,' says I, 'I don't mind if I do.' "

One man winked, and another said: "Go it, Liza!"

She fired up with the dignity of outraged innocence.

"Wot d'yer mean by thet?" she said; "d'yer think I'm kiddin'?"

83

"Kiddin'? No! You've only just come up from the country, ain't yer?"

"Think I'm kidding? What d'yer think I want ter kid for? Liars never believe anyone, thet's fact."

"Na then, Liza, don't be saucy."

"Saucy! I'll smack yer in the eye if yer sy much ter me. Come on," she said to Jim, who had been standing sheepishly by; and they walked away.

The men shouted: "Now we shan't be long!" and went off laughing.

After that they decided to go where there was no chance at all of their being seen. They did not meet till they got over Westminster Bridge, and thence they made their way into the park; they would lie down on the grass in one another's arms, and thus spend the long summer evenings. After the heat of the day there would be a gentle breeze in the park, and they would take in long breaths of the air; it seemed far away from London, it was so quiet and cool; and Liza, as she lay by Jim's side, felt her love for him overflowing to the rest of the world and enveloping mankind itself in a kind of grateful happiness. If it could only have lasted! They would stay and see the stars shine out dimly, one by one, from the blue sky, till it grew late and the blue darkened into black, and the stars glittered in thousands all above them. But as the nights grew cooler, they found it cold on the grass, and the time they had there seemed too short for the long journey they had to make; so, crossing the bridge as before, they strolled along the Embankment till they came to a vacant bench, and there they would sit, with Liza nestling close up to her lover and his great arms around her. The rain of September made no difference to them; they went as usual to their seat beneath the trees, and Jim would take Liza on his knee, and, opening his coat, shelter her with it, while she, with her arms round his neck, pressed very close to him, and occasionally gave a little laugh of pleasure and delight. They hardly spoke at all through these evenings, for what had they to say to one another? Often without exchanging a word they would sit for an hour with their faces touching, the one feeling on his cheek the hot breath from the other's mouth; while at the end of the time the only motion was an upraising of Liza's lips, a bending down of Jim's, so that they might meet and kiss. Sometimes Liza fell into a light doze, and Jim would sit very still for fear of waking her, and when she roused herself she would smile, while he bent down again and kissed her. They were very happy. But the hours passed by so quickly, that Big Ben striking twelve came upon them as a surprise, and unwillingly they got up and made their way homewards; their partings were never ending—each evening Jim refused to let her go from his arms, and tears stood in his eyes at the thought of the separation.

"I'd give somethin'," he would say, "if we could be togither always."

"Never mind, old chap!" Liza would answer, herself half crying, "it can't be 'elped, so we must jolly well lump it."

But notwithstanding all their precautions people in Vere Street appeared to know. First of all Liza noticed that the women did not seem quite so cordial as before, and she often fancied they were talking of her; when she passed by they appeared to look at her, then say something or other, and perhaps burst out laughing; but when she approached they would immediately stop speaking, and keep silence in a rather

awkward, constrained manner. For a long time she was un
willing to believe that there was any change in them, and Jim
who had observed nothing, persuaded her that it was all fancy.
But gradually it became clearer, and Jim had to agree with
her that somehow or other people had found out. Once when
Liza had been talking to Polly, Jim's daughter, Mrs. Blakeston
had called her, and when the girl had come to her mother Liza
saw that she spoke angrily, and they both looked across at her.
When Liza caught Mrs. Blakeston's eye she saw in her face a
surly scowl, which almost frightened her; she wanted to brave
it out, and stepped forward a little to go and speak with the
woman, but Mrs. Blakeston, standing still, looked so angrily at
her that she was afraid to. When she told Jim his face grew
dark, and he said: "Blast the woman! I'll give 'er wot for if
she says anythin' ter you."

"Don't strike 'er, wotever 'appens, will yer, Jim?" said Liza.

"She'd better tike care then!" he answered, and he told her
that lately his wife had been sulking, and not speaking to him.
The previous night, on coming home after the day's work and
bidding her "Good evenin'," she had turned her back on him
without answering.

"Can't you answer when you're spoke to?" he had said.

"Good evenin'," she had replied sulkily, with her back still
turned.

After that Liza noticed that Polly avoided her.

"Wot's up, Polly?" she said to her one day. "You never
speaks now; 'ave you 'ad yer tongue cut aht?"

"Me? I ain't got nothin' ter speak abaht, thet I knows of,"
answered Polly, abruptly walking off. Liza grew very red and
quickly looked to see if anyone had noticed the incident. A

couple of youths, sitting on the pavement, had seen it, and she saw them nudge one another and wink.

Then the fellows about the street began to chaff her.

"You look pale," said one of a group to her one day.

"You're overworkin' yerself, you are," said another.

"Married life don't agree with Liza, thet's wot it is," added a third.

" 'Oo d'yer think yer gettin' at? I ain't married, an' never like ter be," she answered.

"Liza 'as all the pleasures of a 'usband an' none of the trouble."

"Bli'me if I know wot yer mean!" said Liza.

"Na, of course not; you don't know nothin', do yer?"

"Innocent as a bibe. Our Father which art in 'eaven!"

" 'Aven't been in London long, 'ave yer?"

They spoke in chorus, and Liza stood in front of them, bewildered, not knowing what to answer.

"Don't you mike no mistake abaht it, Liza knows a thing or two."

"O me darlin', I love yer fit to kill, but tike care your missus ain't round the corner." This was particularly bold, and they all laughed.

Liza felt very uncomfortable, and fiddled about with her apron, wondering how she should get away.

"Tike care yer don't git into trouble, thet's all," said one of the men, with burlesque gravity.

"Yer might give us a chanst, Liza, you come aht with me one evenin'. You oughter give us all a turn, jist ter show there's no ill-feelin'."

"Bli'me if I know wot yer all talkin' abaht. You're all

barmy on the crumpet," said Liza indignantly, and, turning her back on them, made for home.

Among other things that had happened was Sally's marriage. One Saturday a little procession had started from Vere Street, consisting of Sally, in a state of giggling excitement, her fringe magnificent after a whole week of curling-papers, clad in a perfectly new velveteen dress of the colour known as electric blue; and Harry, rather nervous and ill at ease in the unaccustomed restraint of a collar; these two walked arm-in-arm, and were followed by Sally's mother and uncle, also arm-in-arm, and the procession was brought up by Harry's brother and a friend. They started with a flourish of trumpets and an old boot, and walked down the middle of Vere Street, accompanied by the neighbours' good wishes; but as they got into the Westminster Bridge Road and nearer to the church, the happy couple grew silent, and Harry began to perspire freely, so that his collar gave him perfect torture. There was a public-house just opposite the church, and it was suggested that they should have a drink before going in. As it was a solemn occasion they went into the private bar, and there Sally's uncle, who was a man of means, ordered six pots of beer.

"Feel a bit nervous, 'Arry?" asked his friend.

"Na," said Harry, as if he had been used to getting married every day of his life; "bit warm, thet's all."

"Your very good 'ealth, Sally," said her mother, lifting her mug; "this is the last time as I shall ever address you as miss."

"An' may she be as good a wife as you was," added Sally's uncle.

"Well, I don't think my old man ever 'ad no complaint ter

mike abaht me. I did my duty by 'im, although it's me as says it," answered the good lady.

"Well, mates," said Harry's brother, "I reckon it's abaht time to go in. So 'ere's to the 'ealth of Mr. 'Enry Atkins an' 'is future missus."

"An' God bless 'em!" said Sally's mother.

Then they went into the church, and as they solemnly walked up the aisle a pale-faced young curate came out of the vestry and down to the bottom of the chancel. The beer had had a calming effect on their troubled minds, and both Harry and Sally began to think it rather a good joke. They smiled on each other, and at those parts of the service which they thought suggestive violently nudged one another in the ribs. When the ring had to be produced, Harry fumbled about in different pockets, and his brother whispered:

"Swop me bob, 'e's gone and lorst it!"

However, all went right, and Sally having carefully pocketed the certificate, they went out and had another drink to celebrate the happy event.

In the evening Liza and several friends came into the couple's room, which they had taken in the same house as Sally had lived in before, and drank the health of the bride and bridegroom till they thought fit to retire.

CHAPTER X

IT was November. The fine weather had quite gone now, and with it much of the sweet pleasure of Jim and Liza's love. When they came out at night on the Embankment they found it cold and dreary; sometimes a light fog covered the river-banks, and made the lamps glow out dim and large; a light rain would be falling, which sent a chill into their very souls; foot passengers came along at rare intervals, holding up umbrellas, and staring straight in front of them as they hurried along in the damp and cold; a cab would pass rapidly by, splashing up the mud on each side. The benches were deserted, except, perhaps, for some poor homeless wretch who could afford no shelter, and, huddled up in a corner, with his head buried in his breast, was sleeping heavily, like a dead man. The wet mud made Liza's skirts cling about her feet, and the damp would come in and chill her legs and creep up her body, till she shivered, and for warmth pressed herself close against Jim. Sometimes they would go into the third-class waiting-rooms at Waterloo or Charing Cross and sit there, but it was not like the park or the Embankment on summer nights; they had warmth, but the heat made their wet clothes steam and smell, and the gas flared in their eyes, and they hated the people perpetually coming in and out, opening the doors and letting in a blast of cold air; they hated the noise of the guards and porters shouting out the departure of the trains, the shrill whistling of the steam-engine, the hurry and bustle and con-fusion. About eleven o'clock, when the trains grew less frequent, they got some quietness; but then their minds were troubled, and they felt heavy, sad and miserable.

One evening they had been sitting at Waterloo Station; it was foggy outside—a thick, yellow November fog, which filled the waiting-room, entering the lungs, and making the mouth taste nasty and the eyes smart. It was about half-past eleven, and the station was unusually quiet; a few passengers, in wraps and overcoats, were walking to and fro, waiting for the last train, and one or two porters were standing about yawning. Liza and Jim had remained for an hour in perfect silence, filled with a gloomy unhappiness, as of a great weight on their brains. Liza was sitting forward, with her elbows on her knees, resting her face on her hands.

"I wish I was straight," she said at last, not looking up.

"Well, why won't yer come along of me altogether, an' you'll be arright then?" he answered.

"Na, that's no go; I can't do thet." He had often asked her to live with him entirely, but she had always refused.

"You can come along of me, an' I'll tike a room in a lodgin' 'ouse in 'Olloway, an' we can live there as if we was married."

"Wot abaht yer work?"

"I can get work over the other side as well as I can 'ere. I'm abaht sick of the wy things is goin' on."

"So am I; but I can't leave mother."

"She can come, too."

"Not when I'm not married. I shouldn't like 'er ter know as I'd—as I'd gone wrong."

"Well, I'll marry yer. Swop me bob, I wants ter badly enough."

"Yer can't; yer married already."

"Thet don't matter! If I give the missus so much a week aht of my screw, she'll sign a piper ter give up all clime ter me, an' then we can get spliced. One of the men as I works with done thet, an' it was arright."

Liza shook her head.

"Na, yer can't do thet now; it's bigamy, an' the cop tikes yer, an' yer gits twelve months' 'ard for it."

"But swop me bob, Liza, I can't go on like this. Yer knows the missus—well, there ain't no bloomin' doubt abaht it, she knows as you an' me are carryin' on, an' she mikes no bones abaht lettin' me see it."

"She don't do thet?"

"Well, she don't exactly sy it, but she sulks an' won't speak, an' then when I says anythin' she rounds on me an' calls me all the nimes she can think of. I'd give 'er a good 'idin', but some'ow I don't like ter! She mikes the plice a 'ell ter me, an' I'm not goin' ter stand it no longer!"

"You'll 'ave ter sit it, then; yer can't chuck it."

"Yus I can, an' I would if you'd come along of me. I don't believe you like me at all, Liza, or you'd come."

She turned towards him and put her arms round his neck.

"Yer know I do, old cock," she said. "I like yer better than anyone else in the world; but I can't go awy an' leave mother."

"Bli'me me if I see why; she's never been much ter you. She mikes yer slave awy ter pay the rent, an' all the money she earns she boozes."

"Thet's true, she ain't been wot yer might call a good mother ter me—but some'ow she's my mother, an' I don't like ter leave 'er on 'er own, now she's so old—an' she can't do much with the rheumatics. An' besides, Jim dear, it ain't only mother, but there's yer own kids, yer can't leave them."

He thought for a while, and then said:

"You're abaht right there, Liza; I dunno if I could get on without the kids. If I could only tike them an' you too, swop me bob, I should be 'appy."

Liza smiled sadly.

"So yer see, Jim, we're in a bloomin' 'ole, an' there ain't no way aht of it thet I can see."

He took her on his knees, and pressing her to him, kissed her very long and very lovingly.

"Well, we must trust ter luck," she said again, "p'raps somethin' 'll 'appen soon, an' everythin' 'll come right in the end—when we gets four balls of worsted for a penny."

It was past twelve, and separating, they went by different ways along the dreary, wet, deserted roads till they came to Vere Street.

The street seemed quite different to Liza from what it had been three months before. Tom, the humble adorer, had quite disappeared from her life. One day, three or four weeks after the August Bank Holiday, she saw him dawdling along the pavement, and it suddenly struck her that she had not seen him for a long time; but she had been so full of her happiness that she had been unable to think of anyone but Jim. She wondered at his absence, since before wherever she had been there was he certain to be also. She passed him, but to her astonishment he did not speak to her. She thought by some wonder he had not seen her, but she felt his gaze resting upon her. She turned back, and suddenly he dropped his eyes and looked down, walking on as if he had not seen her, but blushing furiously.

"Tom," she said, "why don't yer speak ter me."

He started and blushed more than ever.

"I didn't know yer **was there**," he stuttered.

"Don't tell me," she said, "wot's up?"

"Nothin' as I knows of," he answered uneasily.

"I ain't offended yer, 'ave I, Tom?"

"Na, not as I knows of," he replied, looking very unhappy.

"You don't ever come my way now," she said.

"I didn't know as yer wanted ter see me."

"Garn! Yer knows I likes you as well as anybody."

"Yer likes so many people, Liza," he said, flushing.

"What d'yer mean?" said Liza indignantly, but very. red; she was afraid he knew now, and it was from him especially she would have been so glad to hide it.

"Nothin'," he answered.

"One doesn't say things like thet without any meanin', unless one's a blimed fool."

"You're right there, Liza," he answered. "I am a blimed fool." He looked at her a little reproachfully, she thought, and then he said "Good-bye," and turned away.

At first she was horrified that he should know of her love for Jim, but then she did not care. After all, it was nobody's business, and what did anything matter as long as she loved Jim and Jim loved her? Then she grew angry that Tom should suspect her; he could know nothing but that some of the men had seen her with Jim near Vauxhall, and it seemed mean that he should condemn her for that. Thenceforward, when she ran against Tom, she cut him; he never tried to speak to her, but as she passed him, pretending to look in front of her, she could see that he always blushed, and she fancied his eyes were very sorrowful. Then several weeks went by, and as she began to feel more and more lonely in the street, she regretted the quarrel; she cried a little as she thought that she had lost his faithful, gentle love, and she would have much liked to be friends with him again. If he had only made some advance she would have welcomed him so cordially, but she was too proud to go to him herself and beg him to forgive her—and then, how could he forgive her?

She had lost Sally too, for on her marriage Harry had made her give up the factory; he was a young man with principles worthy of a Member of Parliament, and he had said:

"A woman's plice is 'er 'ome, an' if 'er old man can't afford ter keep 'er without 'er workin' in a factory—well, all I can say is thet 'e'd better go an' git single."

"Quite right, too," agreed his mother-in-law; "an' wot's more, she'll 'ave a baby ter look after soon, an' thet'll tike 'er all 'er time, an' there's no one as knows thet better than me, for I've 'ad twelve, ter sy nothin' of two stills an' one miss."

Liza quite envied Sally her happiness, for the bride was brimming over with song and laughter; her happiness overwhelmed her.

"I am 'appy," she said to Liza one day a few weeks after her marriage. "You dunno wot a good sort 'Arry is. 'E's just a darlin', an' there's no mistikin' it. I don't care wot other people sy, but wot I says is, there's nothin' like marriage. Never a cross word passes his lips, an' mother 'as all 'er meals with us, an' 'e says all the better. Well, I'm thet 'appy I simply dunno if I'm standin' on my 'ead or on my 'eels."

But alas! it did not last too long. Sally was not so full of joy when next Liza met her, and one day her eyes looked very much as if she had been crying.

"Wot's the matter?" asked Liza, looking at her. "Wot 'ave yer been blubberin' abaht?"

"Me?" said Sally, getting very red. "Oh, I've got a bit of a toothache, an'—well, I'm rather a fool like, an' it 'urt so much that I couldn't 'elp cryin'."

Liza was not satisfied, but could get nothing further out of her. Then one day it came out. It was a Saturday night, the time when women in Vere Street weep. Liza went up into Sally's room for a few minutes on her way to the Westminster Bridge Road, where she was to meet Jim. Harry had taken the top back room, and Liza, climbing up the second flight of stairs, called out as usual,

"Wot ho, Sally!"

The door remained shut, although Liza could see that there was a light in the room; but on getting to the door she stood still, for she heard the sound of sobbing. She listened for a minute and then knocked: there was a little flurry inside, and someone called out:

" 'Oo's there?"

"Only me," said Liza, opening the door. As she did so she saw Sally rapidly wipe her eyes and put her handkerchief away. Her mother was sitting by her side, evidently comforting her.

"Wot's up, Sal?" asked Liza.

"Nothin'," answered Sally, with a brave little gasp to stop the crying, turning her face downwards so that Liza should not see the tears in her eyes; but they were too strong for her, and, quickly taking out her handkerchief, she hid her face in it and began to sob broken-heartedly. Liza looked at the mother in interrogation.

"Oh, it's thet man again!" said the lady, snorting and tossing her head.

"Not 'Arry?" asked Liza, in surprise.

"Not 'Arry—'oo is it if it ain't 'Arry? The villin!"

"Wot's 'e been doin', then?" asked Liza again.

"Beatin' 'er, that's wot 'e's been doin'! Oh, the villin, 'e oughter be ashimed of 'isself, 'e ought!"

"I didn't know 'e was like that!" said Liza.

"Didn't yer? I thought the 'ole street knew it by now," said Mrs. Cooper indignantly. "Oh, 'e's a wrong 'un, 'e is."

"It wasn't 'is fault," put in Sally, amidst her sobs; "it's only because 'e's 'ad a little drop too much. 'E's arright when 'e's sober."

"A little drop too much! I should just think 'e'd 'ad, the beast! I'd give it 'im if I was a man. They're all like thet— 'usbinds is all alike; they're arright when they're sober— sometimes—but when they've got the liquor in 'em, they're beasts, an' no mistike. I 'ad a 'usbind myself for five-an'-twenty years, an' I know 'em."

"Well, mother," sobbed Sally, "it was all my fault. I should 'ave come 'ome earlier."

"Na, it wasn't your fault at all. Just you look 'ere, Liza: this is wot 'e done an' call 'isself a man. Just because Sally'd gone aht to 'ave a chat with Mrs. McLeod in the next 'ouse, when she come in 'e start bangin' 'er abaht. An' me, too, wot d'yer think of that!" Mrs. Cooper was quite purple with indignation.

"Yus," she went on, "thet's a man for yer. Of course, I wasn't goin' ter stand there an' see my daughter bein' knocked abaht; it wasn't likely—was it? An' 'e rounds on me, an' 'e 'its

97

me with 'is fist. Look 'ere." She pulled up her sleeves and showed two red and brawny arms. " 'E's bruised my arms; I thought 'e'd broken it at fust. If I 'adn't put my arm up, 'e'd 'ave got me on the 'ead, an' 'e might 'ave killed me. An' I says to 'im, 'If you touch me again, I'll go ter the police-station, thet I will!' Well, that frightened 'im a bit, an' then didn't I let 'im 'ave it! 'You call yerself a man,' says I, 'an' you ain't fit ter clean the drains aht.' You should 'ave 'eard the language 'e used. 'You dirty old woman,' says 'e, 'you go away; you're always interferin' with me.' Well, I don't like ter repeat wot 'e said, and thet's the truth. An' I says ter 'im, 'I wish yer'd never married my daughter, an' if I'd known you was like this I'd 'ave died sooner than let yer.' "

"Well, I didn't know 'e was like thet!" said Liza.

" 'E was arright at fust," said Sally.

"Yus, they're always arright at fust! But ter think it should 'ave come to this now, when they ain't been married three months, an' the first child not born yet! I think it's disgraceful."

Liza stayed a little while longer, helping to comfort Sally, who kept pathetically taking to herself all the blame of the dispute; and then, bidding her good night and better luck, she slid off to meet Jim.

When she reached the appointed spot he was not to be found. She waited for some time, and at last saw him come out of the neighbouring pub.

"Good night, Jim," she said as she came up to him.

"So you've turned up, 'ave yer?" he answered roughly, turning round.

"Wot's the matter, Jim?" she asked in a frightened way, for he had never before spoken to her in that manner.

"Nice thing ter keep me witin' all night for yer to come aht."

She saw that he had been drinking, and answered humbly:

"I'm very sorry, Jim, but I went in to Sally, an' 'er bloke 'ad been knockin' 'er abaht, an' so I sat with 'er a bit."

"Knockin' 'er abaht, 'ad 'e? and serve 'er damn well right too; an' there's many more as could do with a good 'idin'!"

Liza did not answer. He looked at her, and then suddenly said:

"Come in an' 'ave a drink."

"Na, I'm not thirsty; I don't want a drink," she answered.

"Come on," he said angrily.

"Na, Jim, you've had quite enough already."

" 'Oo are you talkin' ter?" he said. "Don't come if yer don't want ter; I'll go an' 'ave one by myself."

"Na, Jim, don't." She caught hold of his arm.

"Yus, I shall," he said, going towards the pub, while she held him back. "Let me go, can't yer! Let me go!" He roughly pulled his arm away from her. As she tried to catch hold of it again, he pushed her back, and in the little scuffle caught her a blow over the face.

"Oh!" she cried, "you did 'urt!"

He was sobered at once.

"Liza," he said. "I ain't 'urt yer?" She didn't answer, and he took her in his arms. "Liza, I ain't 'urt you, 'ave I? Say I ain't 'urt yer. I'm so sorry, I beg your pardon, Liza."

"Arright, old chap," she said, smiling charmingly on him. "It wasn't the blow that 'urt me much; it was the wy you was talkin'."

"I didn't mean it, Liza." He was so contrite, he could not

humble himself enough. "I 'ad another bloomin' row with the missus ter-night, an' then when I didn't find you 'ere, an' I kept witin' an' witin'—well, I fair downright lost my 'air. An' I 'ad two or three pints of four 'alf, an'—well, I dunno——"

"Mever mind, old cock, I can stand more than thet as long as yer loves me."

He kissed her and they were quite friends again. But the little quarrel had another effect which was worse for Liza. When she woke up next morning she noticed a slight soreness over the ridge of bone under the left eye, and on looking in the glass saw that it was black and blue and green. She bathed it, but it remained, and seemed to get more marked. She was terrified lest people should see it, and kept indoors all day; but next morning it was blacker than ever. She went to the factory with her hat over eyes and her head bent down; she escaped observation, but on the way home she was not so lucky. The sharp eyes of some girls noticed it first.

"Wot's the matter with yer eye?" asked one of them.

"Me?" answered Liza, putting her hand up as if in ignorance. "Nothin' thet I knows of."

Two or three young men were standing by, and hearing the girl, looked up.

"Why, yer've got a black eye, Liza!"

"Me? I ain't got no black eye!"

"Yus, you 'ave; 'ow d'yer get it?"

"I dunno," said Liza. "I didn't know I 'ad one."

"Garn! tell us another!" was the answer. "One doesn't git a black eye without knowin' 'ow they got it."

"Well, I did fall against the chest of drawers yesterday; I suppose I must 'ave got it then."

"Oh yes, we believe thet, don't we?"

"I didn't know 'e was so 'andy with 'is dukes, did you, Ted?" asked one man of another.

Liza felt herself grow red to the tips of her toes.

"Who?" she asked.

"Never you mind; nobody you know."

At that moment Jim's wife passed and looked at her with a scowl. Liza wished herself a hundred miles away, and blushed more violently than ever.

"Wot are yer blushin' abaht?" ingenuously asked one of the girls.

And they all looked from her to Mrs. Blakeston and back again. Someone said: " 'Ow abaht our Sunday boots on now?" And a titter went through them. Liza's nerve deserted her; she could think of nothing to say, and a sob burst from her. To hide the tears which were coming from her eyes she turned away and walked homewards. Immediately a great shout of laughter broke from the group, and she heard them positively screaming till she got into her own house.

CHAPTER XI

A FEW days afterwards Liza was talking with Sally, who did not seem very much happier than when Liza had last seen her.

" 'E ain't wot I thought 'e wos," she said. "1 don't mind sayin' thet; but 'e 'as a lot ter put up with; I expect I'm rather tryin' sometimes, an' 'e means well. P'raps 'e'll be kinder like when the biby's born."

"Cheer up, old gal," answered Liza, who had seen something of the lives of many married couples; "it won't seem so bad after yer gets used to it; it's a bit disappointin' at fust, but yer gits not ter mind it."

After a little Sally said she must go and see about her husband's tea. She said good-bye, and then rather awkwardly:

"Say, Liza, tike care of yerself!"

"Tike care of meself—why?" asked Liza, in surprise.

"Yer know wot I mean."

"Na, I'm darned if I do."

"Thet there Mrs. Blakeston, she's lookin' aht for you."

"Mrs. Blakeston!" Liza was startled.

"Yus; she says she's goin' ter give you somethin' if she can git 'old on yer. I should advise yer ter tike care."

"Me?" said Liza.

Sally looked away, so as not to see the other's face.

"She says as 'ow yer've been messin' abaht with 'er old man."

Liza didn't say anything, and Sally, repeating her good-bye, slid off.

Liza felt a chill run through her. She had several times

noticed a scowl and a look of anger on Mrs. Blakeston's face, and she had avoided her as much as possible; but she had no idea that the woman meant to do anything to her. She was very frightened, a cold sweat broke out over her face. If Mrs. Blakeston got hold of her she would be helpless, she was so small and weak, while the other was strong and muscular. Liza wondered what she would do if she did catch her.

That night she told Jim, and tried to make a joke of it.

"I say, Jim, your missus—she says she's goin' ter give me socks if she catches me."

"My missus! 'Ow d'yer know?"

"She's been tellin' people in the street."

"Go' lumme," said Jim, furious, "if she dares ter touch a 'air of your 'ead, swop me dicky I'll give 'er sich a 'idin' as she never 'ad before! By God, give me the chanst, an' I would let 'er 'ave it; I'm bloomin' well sick of 'er sulks!" He clenched his fist as he spoke.

Liza was a coward. She could not help thinking of her enemy's threat; it got on her nerves, and she hardly dared go out for fear of meeting her; she would look nervously in front of her, quickly turning round if she saw in the distance anyone resembling Mrs. Blakeston. She dreamed of her at night; she saw the big, powerful form, the heavy, frowning face, and the curiously braided brown hair; and she would wake up with a cry and find herself bathed in sweat.

It was the Saturday afternoon following this, a chill November day, with the roads sloshy, and a grey, comfortless sky that made one's spirits sink. It was about three o'clock, and Liza was coming home from work; she got into Vere Street, and was walking quickly towards her house when she saw

Mrs. Blakeston coming towards her. Her heart gave a great jump. Turning, she walked rapidly in the direction she had come; with a screw round of her eyes she saw that she was being followed, and therefore went straight out of Vere Street. She went right round, meaning to get into the street from the other end and, unobserved, slip into her house, which was then quite close; but she dared not risk it immediately for fear Mrs. Blakeston should still be there; so she waited about for half an hour. It seemed an age. Finally, taking her courage in both hands, she turned the corner and entered Vere Street. She nearly ran into the arms of Mrs. Blakeston, who was standing close to the public-house door.

Liza gave a little cry, and the woman said, with a sneer:

"Yer didn't expect ter see me, did yer?"

Liza did not answer, but tried to walk past her. Mrs. Blakeston stepped forward and blocked her way.

"Yer seem ter be in a mighty fine 'urry," she said.

"Yus, I've got ter git 'ome," said Liza, again trying to pass.

"But supposin' I don't let yer?" remarked Mrs. Blakeston, preventing her from moving.

"Why don't yer leave me alone?" Liza said. "I ain't interferin' with you!"

"Not interferin' with me, aren't yer? I like thet!"

"Let me go by," said Liza. "I don't want ter talk ter you."

"Na, I know thet," said the other; "but I want ter talk ter you, an' I shan't let yer go until I've said wot I wants ter sy."

Liza looked round for help. At the beginning of the altercation the loafers about the public-house had looked up with interest, and gradually gathered round in a little circle.

Passers-by had joined in, and a number of other people in the street, seeing the crowd, added themselves to it to see what was going on. Liza saw that all eyes were fixed on her, the men amused and excited, the women unsympathetic, rather virtuously indignant. Liza wanted to ask for help, but there were so many people, and they all seemed so much against her, that she had not the courage to. So, having surveyed the crowd, she turned her eyes to Mrs. Blakeston, and stood in front of her, trembling a little, and very white.

"Na, 'e ain't there," said Mrs. Blakeston, sneeringly, "so yer needn't look for 'im."

"I dunno wot yer mean," answered Liza, "an' I want ter go awy. I ain't done nothin' ter you."

"Not done nothin' ter me?" furiously repeated the woman. "I'll tell yer wot yer've done ter me—you've robbed me of my 'usbind, you 'ave. I never 'ad a word with my 'usbind until you took 'im from me. An' now it's all you with 'im. 'E's got no time for 'is wife an' family—it's all you. An' 'is money, too. I never git a penny of it; if it weren't for the little bit I 'ad saved up in the siving-bank, me an' my children 'ud be starvin' now! An' all through you!" She shook her fist at her.

"I never 'ad any money from anyone."

"Don't talk ter me; I know yer did. Yer dirty bitch! You oughter be ashimed of yourself tikin' a married man from 'is family, an' 'im old enough ter be yer father."

"She's right there!" said one or two of the onlooking women. "There can't be no good in 'er if she tikes somebody else's 'usbind."

"I'll give it yer!" proceeded Mrs. Blakeston, getting more hot and excited, brandishing her fist, and speaking in a loud

105

voice, hoarse with rage. "Oh, I've been tryin' ter git 'old on yer this four weeks. Why, you're a prostitute—thet's wot you are!"

"I'm not!" answered Liza indignantly.

"Yus, you are," repeated Mrs. Blakeston, advancing menacingly, so that Liza shrank back. "An' wot's more, 'e treats yer like one. I know 'oo give yer thet black eye; thet shows what 'e thinks of yer! An' serve yer bloomin' well right if 'e'd give yer one in both eyes!"

Mrs. Blakeston stood close in front of her, her heavy jaw protruded and the frown of her eyebrows dark and stern. For a moment she stood silent, contemplating Liza, while the surrounders looked on in breathless interest.

"Yer dirty little bitch, you!" she said at last. "Tike that!" and with her open hand she gave her a sharp smack on the cheek.

Liza started back with a cry and put her hand up to her face.

"An' tike thet!" added Mrs. Blakeston, repeating the blow. Then, gathering up the spittle in her mouth, she spat in Liza's face.

Liza sprang on her, and with her hands spread out like claws buried her nails in the woman's face and drew them down her cheeks. Mrs. Blakeston caught hold of her hair with both hands and tugged at it as hard as she could. But they were immediately separated.

" 'Ere, 'old 'ard!" said some of the men. "Fight it aht fair and square. Don't go scratchin' and maulin' like thet."

"I'll fight 'er, I don't mind!" shouted Mrs. Blakeston, tucking up her sleeves and savagely glaring at her opponent.

Liza stood in front of her, pale and trembling; as she looked at her enemy, and saw the long red marks of her nails, with blood coming from one or two of them, she shrank back.

"I don't want ter fight," she said hoarsely.

"Na, I don't suppose yer do," hissed the other, "but yer'll damn well 'ave ter!"

"She's ever so much bigger than me; I've got no chanst," added Liza tearfully.

"You should 'ave thought of thet before. Come on!" and with these words Mrs. Blakeston rushed upon her. She hit her with both fists one after the other. Liza did not try to guard herself, but imitating the woman's motion, hit out with her own fists; and for a minute or two they continued thus, raining blows on one another with the same windmill motion of the arms. But Liza could not stand against the other woman's weight; the blows came down heavy and rapid all over her face and head. She put up her hands to cover her face and turned her head away, while Mrs. Blakeston kept on hitting mercilessly.

"Time!" shouted some of the men—"Time!" and Mrs. Blakeston stopped to rest herself.

"It don't seem 'ardly fair to set them two on tergether. Liza's got no chanst against a big woman like thet," said a man among the crowd.

"Well, it's 'er own fault," answered a woman; "she didn't oughter mess about with 'er 'usbind."

"Well, I don't think it's right," added another man. "She's gettin' it too much."

"An' serve 'er right too!" said one of the women. "She deserves all she gets, an' a damn sight more inter the bargain."

"Quite right," put in a third; "a woman's got no right ter

tike someone's 'usbind from 'er. An' if she does she's bloomin' lucky if she gits off with a 'idin'—thet's wot I think."

"So do I. But I wouldn't 'ave thought it of Liza. I never thought she was a wrong 'un."

"Pretty specimen she is!" said a little dark woman, who looked like a Jewess. "If she messed abaht with my old man, I'd stick 'er—I swear I would!"

"Now she's been carryin' on with one, she'll try an' git others—you see if she don't."

"She'd better not come round my 'ouse; I'll soon give 'er wot for."

Meanwhile Liza was standing at one corner of the ring, trembling all over and crying bitterly. One of her eyes was bunged up, and her hair, all dishevelled, was hanging down over her face. Two young fellows, who had constituted themselves her seconds, were standing in front of her, offering rather ironical comfort. One of them had taken the bottom corners of her apron and was fanning her with it, while the other was showing her how to stand and hold her arms.

"You stand up to 'er, Liza," he was saying; "there ain't no good funkin' it, you'll simply get it all the worse. You 'it 'er back. Give 'er one on the boko, like this—see; yer must show a bit of pluck, yer know."

Liza tried to check her sobs.

"Yus, 'it 'er 'ard, that's wot yer've got ter do," said the other. "An' if yer find she's gettin' the better on yer, you close on 'er and catch 'old of 'er 'air and scratch 'er."

"You've marked 'er with yer nails, Liza. By gosh, you did fly on her when she spat at yer! thet's the way ter do the job!"

Then turning to his fellow, he said:

"D'yer remember thet fight as old Mother Gregg 'ad with another woman in the street last year?"

"Na," he answered, "I never saw thet."

"It was a cawker; an' the cops come in and took 'em both off ter quod."

Liza wished the policemen would come and take her off; she would willingly have gone to prison to escape the fiend in front of her; but no help came.

"Time's up!" shouted the referee. "Fire away!"

"Tike care of the cops!" shouted a man.

"There's no fear abaht them," answered somebody else. "They always keeps out of the way when there's anythin' goin' on."

"Fire away!"

Mrs. Blakeston attacked Liza madly; but the girl stood up bravely, and as well as she could gave back the blows she received. The spectators grew tremendously excited.

"Got 'im again!" they shouted. "Give it 'er, Liza, thet's a good 'un!—'it 'er 'ard!"

"Two ter one on the old 'un!" shouted a sporting gentleman; but Liza found no backers.

"Ain't she standin' up well now she's roused?" cried someone.

"Oh, she's got some pluck in 'er, she 'as!"

"Thet's a knock-aht!" they shouted as Mrs. Blakeston brought her fist down on to Liza's nose; the girl staggered back, and blood began to flow. Then, losing all fear, mad with rage, she made a rush on her enemy, and rained down blows all over her nose and eyes and mouth. The woman recoiled at

8

the sudden violence of the onslaught, and the men cried:

"By God, the little 'un's gettin' the best of it!"

But quickly recovering herself the woman closed with Liza, and dug her nails into her flesh. Liza caught hold of her hair and pulled with all her might, and turning her teeth on Mrs. Blakeston tried to bite her. And thus for a minute they swayed about, scratching, tearing, biting, sweat and blood pouring down their faces, and their eyes fixed on one another, bloodshot and full of rage. The audience shouted and cheered and clapped their hands.

"Wot the 'ell's up 'ere?"

"I sy, look there," said some of the women in a whisper. "It's the 'usbind!"

He stood on tiptoe and looked over the crowd.

"My Gawd," he said, "it's Liza!"

Then roughly pushing the people aside, he made his way through the crowd into the centre, and thrusting himself between the two women, tore them apart. He turned furiously on his wife.

"By Gawd, I'll give yer somethin' for this!"

And for a moment they all three stood silently looking at one another.

Another man had been attracted by the crowd, and he, too, pushed his way through.

"Come 'ome, Liza," he said.

"Tom!"

He took hold of her arm, and led her through the people, who gave way to let her pass. They walked silently through the street, Tom very grave. Liza weeping bitterly.

"Oh, Tom," she sobbed after a while, "I couldn't 'elp

it!" Then, when her tears permitted, "I did love 'im so!"

When they got to the door she plaintively said: "Come in," and he followed her to her room. Here she sank on to a chair, and gave herself up to her tears.

Tom wetted the end of a towel and began wiping her face, grimy with blood and tears. She let him do it, just moaning amid her sobs:

"You are good ter me, Tom."

"Cheer up, old gal," he said kindly, "it's all over now."

After a while the excess of crying brought its cessation. She drank some water, and then taking up a broken hand-glass she looked at herself, saying:

"I am a sight!" and proceeded to wind up her hair. "You 'ave been good ter me, Tom," she repeated, her voice still broken with sobs; and as he sat down beside her she took his hand.

"Na, I ain't," he answered; "it's only wot anybody 'ud 'ave done."

"Yer know, Tom," she said, after a little silence, "I'm so sorry I spoke cross like when I met yer in the street; you ain't spoke ter me since."

"Oh, thet's all over now, old lidy, we needn't think of thet."

"Oh, but I 'ave treated yer bad. I'm a regular wrong 'un, I am."

He pressed her hand without speaking.

"I say, Tom," she began, after another pause. "Did yer know thet—well, you know—before ter-day?"

He blushed as he answered:

"Yus."

She spoke very sadly and slowly.

111

"I thought yer did; yer seemed so cut up like when I used to meet yer. Yer did love me then, Tom, didn't yer?"

"I do now, dearie," he answered.

"Ah, it's too lite now," she sighed.

"D'yer know, Liza," he said, "I just abaht kicked the life aht of a feller 'cause 'e said you was messin' abaht with—with 'im.'"

"An' yer knew I was?"

"Yus—but I wasn't goin' ter 'ave anyone say it before me."

"They've all rounded on me except you, Tom. I'd 'ave done better if I'd tiken you when you arst me; I shouldn't be where I am now, if I 'ad."

"Well, won't yer now? Won't yer 'ave me now?"

"Me? After wot's 'appened?"

"Oh, I don't mind abaht thet. Thet don't matter ter me if you'll marry me. I fair can't live without yer, Liza—won't yer?"

She groaned.

"Na, I can't, Tom, it wouldn't be right."

"Why, not, if I don't mind?"

"Tom," she said, looking down, almost whispering, "I'm like that—you know!"

"Wot d'yer mean?"

She could scarcely utter the words—

"I think I'm in the family wy."

He paused a moment; then spoke again.

"Well—I don't mind, if yer'll only marry me."

"Na, I can't, Tom," she said, bursting into tears; "I can't, but you are so good ter me; I'd do anythin' ter mike it up ter you."

She put her arms round his neck and slid on to his knees.

"Yer know, Tom, I couldn't marry yer now; but anythin' else—if yer wants me ter do anythin' else, I'll do it if it'll mike you 'appy."

He did not understand, but only said:

"You're a good gal, Liza," and bending down he kissed her gravely on the forehead.

Then with a sigh he lifted her down, and getting up left her alone. For a while she sat where he left her, but as she thought of all she had gone through her loneliness and misery overcame her, the tears welled forth, and throwing herself on the bed she buried her face in the pillows.

Jim stood looking at Liza as she went off with Tom, and his wife watched him jealously.

"It's 'er you're thinkin' abaht. Of course you'd 'ave liked ter tike 'er 'ome yerself, I know, an' leave me to shift for myself."

"Shut up!" said Jim, angrily turning upon her.

"I shan't shut up," she answered, raising her voice. "Nice 'usbind you are. Go' lumme, as good as they mike 'em! Nice thing ter go an' leave yer wife and children for a thing like thet! At your age, too! You oughter be ashimed of yerself. Why, it's like messin' abaht with yer own daughter!"

"By God!"—he ground his teeth with rage—"if yer don't leave me alone, I'll kick the life aht of yer!"

"There!" she said, turning to the crowd—"there, see 'ow 'e treats me! Listen ter that! I've been 'is wife for twenty years, an' yer couldn't 'ave 'ad a better wife, an' I've bore 'im nine children, yet say nothin' of a miscarriage, an' I've got

113

another one comin', an' thet's 'ow 'e treats me! Nice 'usbind, ain't it?" She looked at him scornfully, then again at the surrounders as if for their opinion.

"Well, I ain't goin' ter stay 'ere all night; get aht of the light!" He pushed aside the people who barred his way, and the one or two who growled a little at his roughness, looking at his angry face, were afraid to complain.

"Look at 'im!" said his wife. " 'E's afraid, 'e is. See 'im slinkin' awy like a bloomin' mongrel with 'is tail between 'is legs. Ugh!" She walked just behind him, shouting and brandishing her arms.

"Yer dirty beast, you," she yelled, "ter go foolin' abaht with a little girl! Ugh! I wish yer wasn't my 'usbind; I wouldn't be seen drowned with yer, if I could 'elp it. Yer mike me sick ter look at yer."

The crowd followed them on both sides of the road, keeping at a discreet distance, but still eagerly listening.

Jim turned on her once or twice and said:

"Shut up!"

But it only made her more angry. "I tell yer I shan't shut up. I don't care 'oo knows it, you're a——, you are! I'm ashimed the children should 'ave such a father as you. D'yer think I didn't know wot you was up ter them nights you was awy—courtin', yus, courtin'? You're a nice man, you are!"

Jim did not answer her, but walked on. At last he turned round to the people who were following and said:

"Na then, wot d'you want 'ere? You jolly well clear, or I'll give some of you somethin'!"

They were mostly boys and women, and at his words they shrank back.

" 'E's afraid ter sy anythin' ter me," jeered Mrs. Blakeston. " 'E's a beauty!"

Jim entered his house, and she followed him till they came up into their room. Polly was giving the children their tea. They all started up as they saw their mother with her hair and clothes in disorder, blotches of dried blood on her face, and the long scratch-marks.

"Oh, mother," said Polly, "wot is the matter?"

" 'E's the matter," she answered, pointing to her husband. "It's through 'im I've got all this. Look at yer father, children; e's a father to be proud of, leavin' yer ter starve an' spendin' 'is week's money on a dirty little strumper."

Jim felt easier now he had not got so many strange eyes on him.

"Now, look 'ere," he said, "I'm not goin' ter stand this much longer, so just you tike care."

"I ain't frightened of yer. I know yer'd like ter kill me, but yer'll get strung up if you do."

"Na, I won't kill yer, but if I 'ave any more of your sauce I'll do the next thing to it."

"Touch me if yer dare," she said, "I'll 'ave the law on you. An' I shouldn't mind 'ow many month's 'ard you got."

"Be quiet!" he said, and, closing his hand, gave her a heavy blow in the chest that made her stagger.

"Oh, you —— !" she screamed.

She seized the poker, and in a fury of rage rushed at him.

"Would yer?" he said, catching hold of it and wrenching it from her grasp. He threw it to the end of the room and grappled with her. For a moment they swayed about from side to side, then with an effort he lifted her off her feet and

115

threw her to the ground; but she caught hold of him and he came down on the top of her. She screamed as her head thumped down on the floor, and the children, who were standing huddled up in a corner, terrified, screamed too.

Jim caught hold of his wife's head and began beating it against the floor.

She cried out: "You're killing me! Help! help!"

Polly in terror ran up to her father and tried to pull him off.

"Father, don't 'it 'er! Anythin' but thet—for God's sike!"

"Leave me alone," he said, "or I'll give you somethin' too."

She caught hold of his arm, but Jim, still kneeling on his wife, gave Polly a backhanded blow which sent her staggering back.

"Tike that!"

Polly ran out of the room, downstairs to the first-floor front, where two men and two women were sitting at tea.

"Oh, come an' stop father!" she cried. " 'E's killin' mother!"

"Why, wot's 'e doin'?"

"Oh, 'e's got 'er on the floor, an' 'e's bangin' 'er 'ead. 'E's payin' 'er aht for givin' Liza Kemp a 'idin'."

One of the women started up and said to her husband:

"Come on, John, you go an' stop it."

"Don't you, John," said the other man. "When a man's givin' 'is wife socks it's best not ter interfere."

"But 'e's killin' 'er," repeated Polly, trembling with fright.

"Garn!" rejoined the man, "she'll git over it; an' p'raps she deserves it, for all you know."

John sat undecided, looking now at Polly, now at his wife, and now at the other man.

116

"Oh, do be quick—for God's sike!" said Polly.

At that moment a sound as of something smashing was heard upstairs, and a woman's shriek. Mrs. Blakeston, in an effort to tear herself away from her husband, had knocked up against the wash-hand stand, and the whole thing had crashed down.

"Go on, John," said the wife.

"No, I ain't goin'; I shan't do no good, an' 'e'll only round on me."

"Well, you are a bloomin' lot of cowards, thet's all I can say," indignantly answered the wife. "But I ain't goin' ter see a woman murdered; I'll go an' stop 'im."

With that she ran upstairs and threw open the door. Jim was still kneeling on his wife, hitting her furiously, while she was trying to protect her head and face with her hands.

"Leave off!" shouted the woman.

Jim looked up. " 'Oo the devil are you?" he said.

"Leave off, I tell yer. Aren't yer ashimed of yerself, knockin' a woman abaht like that?" And she sprang at him, seizing his fist.

"Let go," he said, "or I'll give you a bit."

"Yer'd better not touch me," she said. "Yer dirty coward! Why, look at 'er, she's almost senseless."

Jim stopped and gazed at his wife. He got up and gave her a kick.

"Git up!" he said; but she remained huddled up on the floor, moaning feebly. The woman from downstairs went on her knees and took her head in her arms.

"Never mind, Mrs. Blakeston. 'E's not goin' ter touch yer. 'Ere, drink this little drop of water." Then turning to Jim,

117

with infinite disdain: "Yer dirty blackguard, you! If I was a man I'd give you something for this."

Jim put on his hat and went out, slamming the door, while the woman shouted after him: "Good riddance!"

"Lord love yer," said Mrs. Kemp, "wot is the matter?"

She had just come in, and opening the door had started back in surprise at seeing Liza on the bed, all tears. Liza made no answer, but cried as if her heart were breaking. Mrs. Kemp went up to her and tried to look at her face.

"Don't cry, dearie; tell us wot it is."

Liza sat up and dried her eyes.

"I am so un'appy!"

"Wot 'ave yer been doin' ter yer fice? My!"

"Nothin'."

"Garn! Yer can't 'ave got a fice like thet all by itself."

"I 'ad a bit of a scrimmage with a woman dahn the street," sobbed out Liza.

"She 'as give yer a doin'; an' yer all upset—an' look at yer eye! I brought in a little bit of stike for ter-morrer's dinner; you just cut a bit off an' put it over yer optic, that'll soon put it right. I always used ter do thet myself when me an' your poor father 'ad words."

"Oh, I'm all over in a tremble, an' my 'ead, oo, my 'ead does feel bad!"

"I know wot yer want," remarked Mrs. Kemp, nodding her head, "an' it so 'appens as I've got the very thing with me." She pulled a medicine bottle out of her pocket, and taking out the cork smelt it. "Thet's good stuff, none of your fire-water or your methylated spirit. I don't often indulge in sich things, but when I do I likes to 'ave the best."

She handed the bottle to Liza, who took a mouthful and gave it her back; she had a drink herself, and smacked her lips.

"Thet's good stuff. 'Ave a drop more."

"Na," said Liza, "I ain't used ter drinkin' spirits."

She felt dull and miserable, and a heavy pain throbbed through her head. If she could only forget!

"Na, I know you're not, but, bless your soul, thet won' 'urt yer. It'll do you no end of good. Why, often when I've been feelin' thet done up thet I didn't know wot ter do with myself, I've just 'ad a little drop of whisky or gin—I'm not partic'ler wot spirit it is—an' it's pulled me up wonderful."

Liza took another sip, a slightly longer one; it burnt as it went down her throat, and sent through her a feeling of comfortable warmth.

"I really do think it's doin' me good," she said, wiping her eyes and giving a sigh of relief as the crying ceased.

"I knew it would. Tike my word for it, if people took a little drop of spirits in time, there'd be much less sickness abaht."

They sat for a while in silence, then Mrs. Kemp remarked:

"Yer know, Liza, it strikes me as 'ow we could do with a drop more. You not bein' in the 'abit of tikin' anythin' I only brought just this little drop for me; an' it ain't took us long ter finish thet up. But as you're an invalid like we'll git a little more this time; it's sure ter turn aht useful."

"But you ain't got nothin' ter put it in."

"Yus, I 'ave," answered Mrs. Kemp; "there's thet bottle as they gives me at the 'orspital. Just empty the medicine aht into the pile, an' wash it aht, an' I'll tike it round to the pub myself."

119

Liza, when she was left alone, began to turn things over in her mind. She did not feel so utterably unhappy as before, for the things she had gone through seemed further away.

"After all," she said, "it don't so much matter."

Mrs. Kemp came in.

"'Ave a little drop more, Liza," she said.

"Well, I don't mind if I do. I'll get some tumblers, shall I? There's no mistike abaht it," she added, when she had taken a little, "it do buck yer up."

"You're right, Liza—you're right. An' you wanted it badly, Fancy you 'avin' a fight with a woman! Oh, I've 'ad some in my day, but then I wasn't a little bit of a thing like you is. I wish I'd been there, I wouldn't 'ave stood by an' looked on while my daughter was gettin' the worst of it; although I'm turned sixty-five, an' gettin' on for sixty-six, I'd 'ave said to 'er: 'If you touch my daughter you'll 'ave me ter deal with, so just look aht!' "

She brandished her glass, and that reminding her, she refilled it and Liza's.

"Ah, Liza," she remarked, "you're a chip of the old block. Ter see you settin' there an' 'avin' your little drop, it mikes me feel as if I was livin' a better life. Yer used ter be rather 'ard on me, Liza, 'cause I took a little drop on Saturday nights. An, mind, I don't sy I didn't tike a little drop too much some-times—accidents will occur even in the best regulated of families, but wot I say is this—it's good stuff, I say, an' it don't 'urt yer."

"Buck up, old gal!" said Liza, filling the glasses, "no 'eel-taps. I feel like a new woman now. I was thet dahn in the dumps—well, I shouldn't 'ave cared if I'd been at the bottom of the river, an' thet's the truth."

"You don't sy so," replied her affectionate mother.

"Yus, I do, an' I mean it too, but I don't feel like thet now. You're right, mother, when you're in trouble there's nothin' like a bit of spirits."

"Well, if I don't know, I dunno 'oo does, for the trouble I've 'ad, it 'ud be enough to kill many women. Well, I've 'ad thirteen children, an' you can think wot thet was; everyone I 'ad I used ter sy I wouldn't 'ave no more—but one does, yer know. You'll 'ave a family some day, Liza, an' I shouldn't wonder if you didn't 'ave as many as me. We come from a very prodigal family, we do, we've all gone in ter double figures, except your Aunt Mary, who only 'ad three—but then she wasn't married, so it didn't count, like."

They drank each other's health. Everything was getting blurred to Liza, she was losing her head.

"Yus," went on Mrs. Kemp, "I've 'ad thirteen children an' I'm proud of it. As your poor dear father used ter sy, it shows as 'ow one's got the blood of a Briton in one. Your poor dear father, 'e was a great 'and at speakin' 'e was: 'e used ter speak at parliamentary meetin's—I really believe 'e'd 'ave been a Member of Parliament if 'e'd been alive now. Well, as I was sayin', your father 'e used ter sy, 'None of your small families for me, I don't approve of them,' says 'e. 'E was a man of very 'igh principles, an' by politics 'e was a Radical. 'No,' says 'e, when 'e got talkin', 'when a man can 'ave a family risin' into double figures, it shows 'e's got the backbone of a Briton in 'im. That's the stuff as 'as built up England's nime and glory! When one thinks of the mighty British Hempire,' says 'e, 'on which the sun never sets from mornin' till night, one 'as ter be

121

proud of 'isself, an' one 'as ter do one's duty in thet walk of life in which it 'as pleased Providence ter set one—an' every man's fust duty is ter get as many children as 'e bloomin' well can.' Lord love yer—'e could talk, I can tell yer."

"Drink up, mother," said Liza. "You're not 'alf drinkin'." She flourished the bottle. "I don't care a twopenny 'ang for all them blokes; I'm quite 'appy, an' I don't want anythin' else."

"I can see you're my daughter now," said Mrs. Kemp. "When yer used ter round on me I used ter think as 'ow if I 'adn't carried yer for nine months, it must 'ave been some mistike, an' yer wasn't my daughter at all. When you come ter think of it, a man 'e don't know if it's 'is child or somebody else's, but yer can't deceive a woman like thet. Yer couldn't palm off somebody else's kid on 'er."

"I am beginnin' ter feel quite lively," said Liza. "I dunno wot it is, but I feel as if I wanted to laugh till I fairly split my sides."

And she began to sing: "For 'e's a jolly good feller—for 'e's a jolly good feller!"

Her dress was all disarranged; her face covered with the scars of scratches, and clots of blood had fixed under her nose; her eye had swollen up so that it was nearly closed, and red; her hair was hanging over her face and shoulders, and she laughed stupidly and leered with heavy, sodden ugliness.

> "Disy, Disy! I can't afford a kerridge,
> But you'll look neat, on the seat
> Of a bicycle mide for two."

She shouted out the tunes, beating time on the table, and

her mother, grinning, with her thin, grey hair hanging dishevelled over her head, joined in with her weak, cracked voice—

"Oh, dem golden kippers, oh!"

Then Liza grew more melancholy and broke into "Auld Lang Syne".

"Should old acquaintance be forgot
And never brought to mind?

.   .   .   .

For old lang syne".

Finally they both grew silent, and in a little while there came a snore from Mrs. Kemp; her head fell forward to her chest; Liza tumbled from her chair on to the bed, and sprawling across it fell asleep.

"*Although I am drunk and bad, be you kind,
Cast a glance at this heart which is bewildered and distressed.
O God, take away from my mind my cry and my complaint.
Offer wine, and take sorrow from my remembrance.
Offer wine.*"

CHAPTER XII

ABOUT the middle of the night Liza woke; her mouth was hot and dry, and a sharp, cutting pain passed through her head as she moved. Her mother had evidently roused herself, for she was lying in bed by her side, partially undressed, with all the bedclothes rolled round her. Liza shivered in the cold night, and taking off some of her things—her boots, her skirt, and jacket—got right into bed; she tried to get some of the blanket from her mother, but as she pulled Mrs. Kemp gave a growl in her sleep and drew the clothes more tightly round her. So Liza put over herself her skirt and a shawl, which was lying over the end of the bed, and tried to go to sleep.

But she could not; her head and hands were broiling hot, and she was terribly thirsty; when she lifted herself up to get a drink of water such a pang went through her head that she fell back on the bed groaning, and lay there with beating heart. And strange pains that she did not know went through her. Then a cold shiver seemed to rise in the very marrow of her bones and run down every artery and vein, freezing the blood; her skin puckered up, and drawing up her legs she lay huddled together in a heap, the shawl wrapped tightly round her, and her teeth chattering. Shivering, she whispered:

"Oh, I'm so cold, so cold. Mother, give me some clothes; I shall die of the cold. Oh, I'm freezing!"

But after a while the cold seemed to give way, and a sudden heat seized her, flushing her face, making her break out into perspiration, so that she threw everything off and loosened the things about her neck.

"Give us a drink," she said. "Oh, I'd give anythin' for a little drop of water!"

There was no one to hear; Mrs. Kemp continued to sleep heavily, occasionally breaking out into a little snore.

Liza remained there, now shivering with cold, now panting for breath, listening to the regular, heavy breathing by her side, and in her pain she sobbed. She pulled at her pillow and said:

"Why can't I go to sleep? Why can't I sleep like 'er?"

And the darkness was awful; it was a heavy, ghastly blackness, that seemed palpable, so that it frightened her, and she looked for relief at the faint light glimmering through the window from a distant street-lamp. She thought the night would never end—the minutes seemed like hours, and she wondered how she should live through till morning. And strange pains that she did not know went through her.

Still the night went on, the darkness continued, cold and horrible, and her mother breathed loudly and steadily by her side.

At last with the morning sleep came; but the sleep was almost worse than the wakefulness, for it was accompanied by ugly, disturbing dreams. Liza thought she was going through the fight with her enemy, and Mrs. Blakeston grew enormous in size, and multiplied, so that every way she turned the figure confronted her. And she began running away, and she ran and ran till she found herself reckoning up an account she had puzzled over in the morning, and she did it backwards and forwards, upwards and downwards, starting here, starting there, and the figures got mixed up with other things, and she had to begin over again, and everything jumbled up, and her head whirled, till finally, with a start, she woke.

9

The darkness had given way to a cold, grey dawn, her uncovered legs were chilled to the bone, and by her side she heard again the regular, nasal breathing of the drunkard.

For a long while she lay where she was, feeling very sick and ill, but better than in the night. At last her mother woke.

"Liza!" she called.

"Yus, mother," she answered feebly.

"Git us a cup of tea, will yer?"

"I can't, mother, I'm ill."

"Garn!" said Mrs. Kemp, in surprise. Then looking at her: "Swop me bob, wot's up with yer? Why, yer cheeks is flushed, an' yer forehead—it is 'ot! Wot's the matter with yer, gal?"

"I dunno," said Liza. "I've been thet bad all night, I thought I was goin' ter die."

"I know wot it is," said Mrs. Kemp, shaking her head; "the fact is, you ain't used ter drinkin', an' of course it's upset yer. Now me, why I'm as fresh as a disy. Tike my word, there ain't no good in teetotalism; it finds yer aht in the end, an' it's found you aht."

Mrs. Kemp considered it a judgment of Providence. She got up and mixed some whisky and water.

" 'Ere, drink this," she said. "When one's 'ad a drop too much at night, there's nothin' like havin' a drop more in the mornin' ter put one right. It just acts like magic."

"Tike it awy," said Liza, turning from it in digust; "the smell of it gives me the sick. I'll never touch spirits again."

"Ah, thet's wot we all says sometime in our lives, but we does, an' wot's more we can't do withaht it. Why, me, the 'ard life I've 'ad——" It is unnecessary to repeat Mrs. Kemp's repetitions.

Liza did not get up all day. Tom came to inquire after her, and was told she was very ill. Liza plaintively asked whether anyone else had been, and sighed a little when her mother answered no. But she felt too ill to think much or trouble much about anything. The fever came again as the day wore on, and the pains in her head grew worse. Her mother came to bed, and quickly went off to sleep, leaving Liza to bear her agony alone. She began to have frightful pains all over her, and she held her breath to prevent herself from crying out and waking her mother. She clutched the sheets in her agony, and at last, about six o'clock in the morning, she could bear it no longer, and in the anguish of labour screamed out, and woke her mother.

Mrs. Kemp was frightened out of her wits. Going upstairs she woke the woman who lived on the floor above her. Without hesitating, the good lady put on a skirt and came down.

"She's 'ad a miss," she said, after looking at Liza. "Is there anyone you could send to the 'orspital?"

"Na, I dunno 'oo I could get at this hour?"

"Well, I'll git my old man ter go."

She called her husband, and sent him off. She was a stout, middle-aged woman, rough-visaged and strong-armed. Her name was Mrs. Hodges.

"It's lucky you came ter me," she said, when she had settled down. "I go aht nursin', yer know, so I know all abaht it."

"Well, you surprise me," said Mrs. Kemp. "I didn't know as Liza was thet way. She never told me nothin' abaht it."

"D'yer know 'oo it is 'as done it?"

"Now you ask me somethin' I don't know," replied Mrs. Kemp. "But now I come ter think of it, it must be thet there

127

Tom. 'E's been keepin' company with Liza. 'E's a single man, so they'll be able ter get married—thet's somethin'."

"It ain't Tom," feebly said Liza.

"Not 'im; 'oo is it, then?"

Liza did not answer.

"Eh?" repeated the mother, " 'oo is it?"

Liza lay still without speaking.

"Never mind, Mrs. Kemp," said Mrs. Hodges, "don't worry 'er now; you'll be able ter find aht all abaht it when she gits better."

For a while the two women sat still, waiting the doctor's coming, and Liza lay gazing vacantly at the wall, panting for breath. Sometimes Jim crossed her mind, and she opened her mouth to call for him, but in her despair she restrained herself.

The doctor came.

"D'you think she's bad, doctor?" asked Mrs. Hodges.

"I'm afraid she is rather," he answered. "I'll come in again this evening."

"Oh, doctor," said Mrs. Kemp, as he was going, "could yer give me somethin' for my rheumatics? I'm a martyr to rheumatism, an' these cold days I 'ardly knows wot ter do with myself. An', doctor, could you let me 'ave some beef-tea? My 'usbind's dead, an' of course I can't do no work with my daughter ill like this, an' we're very short——"

The day passed, and in the evening Mrs. Hodges, who had been attending to her own domestic duties, came downstairs again. Mrs. Kemp was on the bed sleeping.

"I was just 'avin' a little nap," she said to Mrs. Hodges, on waking.

" 'Ow is the girl?" asked that lady.

"Oh," answered Mrs. Kemp, "my rheumatics 'as been thet bad I really 'aven't known wot ter do with myself, an' now Liza can't rub me I'm worse than ever. It is unfortunate thet she should get ill just now when I want so much attendin' ter myself, but there, it's just my luck!"

Mrs. Hodges went over and looked at Liza; she was lying just as when she left in the morning, her cheeks flushed, her mouth open for breath, and tiny beads of sweat stood on her forehead.

" 'Ow are yer, ducky?" asked Mrs. Hodges; but Liza did not answer.

"It's my belief she's unconscious," said Mrs. Kemp. "I've been askin' 'er 'oo it was as done it, but she don't seem to 'ear wot I say. It's been a great shock ter me, Mrs. 'Odges."

"I believe you," replied that lady, sympathetically.

"Well, when you come in and said wot it was, yer might 'ave knocked me dahn with a feather. I knew no more than the dead wot 'ad 'appened."

"I saw at once wot it was," said Mrs. Hodges, nodding her head.

"Yus, of course, you knew. I expect you've 'ad a great deal of practice one way an' another."

"You're right, Mrs. Kemp, you're right. I've been on the job now for nearly twenty years, an' if I don't know somethin' abaht it I ought."

"D'yer finds it pays well?"

"Well, Mrs. Kemp, tike it all in all, I ain't got no grounds for complaint. I'm in the 'abit of askin' five shillings, an' I will say this, I don't think it's too much for wot I do."

The news of Liza's illness had quickly spread, and more than once in the course of the day a neighbour had come to ask after her. There was a knock at the door now, and Mrs. Hodges opened it. Tom stood on the threshold asking to come in.

"Yus, you can come," said Mrs. Kemp.

He advanced on tiptoe, so as to make no noise, and for a while stood silently looking at Liza. Mrs. Hodges was by his side.

"Can I speak to 'er?" he whispered.

"She can't 'ear you."

He groaned.

"D'yer think she'll get arright?" he asked.

Mrs. Hodges shrugged her shoulders.

"I shouldn't like ter give an opinion," she said, cautiously.

Tom bent over Liza, and, blushing, kissed her; then, without speaking further, went out of the room.

"Thet's the young man as was courtin' 'er," said Mrs. Kemp, pointing over her shoulder with her thumb.

Soon after the Doctor came.

"Wot do yer think of 'er, doctor?" said Mrs. Hodges, bustling forwards authoritatively in her position of midwife and sick-nurse.

"I'm afraid she's very bad."

"D'yer think she's goin' ter die?" she asked, dropping her voice to a whisper.

"I'm afraid so!"

As the doctor sat down by Liza's side Mrs. Hodges turned round and significantly nodded to Mrs. Kemp, who put her handkerchief to her eyes. Then she went outside to the little group waiting at the door.

"Wot does the doctor sy?" they asked, among them Tom.

" 'E says just wot I've been sayin' all along; I knew she wouldn't live."

And Tom burst out: "Oh, Liza!"

As she retired a woman remarked:

"Mrs. 'Odges is very clever, I think."

"Yus," remarked another, "she got me through my last confinement simply wonderful. If it come to choosin' between 'em I'd back Mrs. 'Odges against forty doctors."

"Ter tell yer the truth, so would I. I've never known 'er wrong yet."

Mrs. Hodges sat down beside Mrs. Kemp and proceeded to comfort her.

"Why don't yer tike a little drop of brandy ter calm yer nerves, Mrs. Kemp?" she said, "you want it."

"I was just feelin' rather faint, an' I couldn't 'elp thinkin' as 'ow twopenneth of whisky 'ud do me good."

"Na, Mrs. Kemp," said Mrs. Hodges, earnestly, putting her hand on the other's arm. "You tike my tip—when you're queer there's nothin' like brandy for pullin' yer togither. I don't object to whisky myself, but as a medicine yer can't beat brandy."

"Well, I won't set up myself as knowin' better than you Mrs. 'Odges; I'll do wot you think right."

Quite accidentally there was some in the room, and Mrs. Kemp poured it out for herself and her friend.

"I'm not in the 'abit of tikin' anythin' when I'm aht on business," she apologised, "but just ter keep you company I don't mind if I do."

"Your 'ealth, Mrs. 'Odges."

"Sime ter you, an' thank yer, Mrs. Kemp."

Liza lay still, breathing very quietly, her eyes closed. The doctor kept his fingers on her pulse.

"I've been very unfortunate of lite," remarked Mrs. Hodges, as she licked her lips, "this mikes the second death I've 'ad in the last ten days—women, I mean, of course I don't count bibies."

"Yer don't sy so."

"Of course the other one—well, she was only a prostitute, so it didn't so much matter. It ain't like another woman, is it?"

"Na, you're right."

"Still, one don't like 'em ter die, even if they are thet. One mustn't be too 'ard on 'em."

"Strikes me you've got a very kind 'eart, Mrs. 'Odges," said Mrs. Kemp.

"I 'ave thet; an' I often says it 'ud be better for my peace of mind an' my business if I 'adn't. I 'ave ter go through a lot, I do; but I can say this for myself, I always gives satisfaction, an' thet's somethin' as all lidies in my line can't say."

They sipped their brandy for a while.

"It's a great trial ter me that this should 'ave 'appened," said Mrs. Kemp, coming to the subject that had been disturbing her for some time. "Mine's always been a very respectable family, an' such a thing as this 'as never 'appened before. No, Mrs. 'Odges, I was lawfully married in church, an' I've got my marriage lines now ter show I was, an' thet one of my daughters should 'ave gone wrong in this way—well, I can't understand it. I give 'er a good education, an' she 'ad all the comforts of a 'ome. She never wanted for nothin'; I worked myself to the bone ter keep 'er in luxury, an' then thet she should go an' disgrace me like this!"

"I understand wot yer mean, Mrs. Kemp."

"I can tell you my family was very respectable; an' my 'usbind, 'e earned twenty-five shillings a week, an' was in the sime plice seventeen years; an' 'is employers sent a beautiful wreath ter put on 'is coffin; an' they tell me they never 'ad such a good workman an' sich an 'onest man before. An' me! Well, I can sy this—I've done my duty by the girl, an' she's never learnt anythin' but good from me. Of course I ain't always been in wot yer might call flourishing circumstances, but I've always set her a good example, as she could tell yer so 'erself if she wasn't speechless."

Mrs. Kemp paused for a moment's reflection.

"As they sy in the Bible," she finished, "it's enough ter mike one's grey 'airs go dahn into the ground in sorrer. I can show yer my marriage certificate. Of course one doesn't like ter say much, because of course she's very bad; but if she got well I should 'ave given 'er a talkin' ter."

There was another knock.

"Do go an' see 'oo thet is; I can't, on account of my rheumatics."

Mrs. Hodges opened the door. It was Jim.

He was very white, and the blackness of his hair and beard, contrasting with the deathly pallor of his face, made him look ghastly. Mrs. Hodges stepped back.

" 'Oo's 'e?" she said, turning to Mrs. Kemp.

Jim pushed her aside and went up to the bed.

"Doctor, is she very bad?" he asked.

The doctor looked at him questioningly.

Jim whispered: "It was me as done it. She ain't goin' ter die, is she?"

133

The doctor nodded.

"O God! wot shall I do? It was my fault! I wish I was dead!"

Jim took the girl's head in his hands, and the tears burst from his eyes.

"She ain't dead yet, is she?"

"She's just living," said the doctor.

Jim bent down.

"Liza, Liza, speak ter me! Liza, say you forgive me! Oh, speak ter me!"

His voice was full of agony. The doctor spoke.

"She can't hear you."

"Oh, she must hear me! Liza! Liza!"

He sank on his knees by the bedside.

They all remained silent: Liza lying stiller than ever, her breast unmoved by the feeble respiration, Jim looking at her very mournfully; the doctor grave, with his fingers on the pulse. The two women looked at Jim.

"Fancy it bein' 'im!" said Mrs Kemp. "Strike me lucky, ain't 'e a sight!"

"You 'ave got 'er insured, Mrs. Kemp?" asked the midwife. She could bear the silence no longer.

"Trust me fur thet!" replied the good lady. "I've 'ad 'er insured ever since she was born. Why, only the other dy I was sayin' ter myself thet all thet money 'ad been wisted, but you see it wasn't; yer never know yer luck, you see!"

"Quite right, Mrs. Kemp; I'm a rare one for insurin'. It's a great thing. I've always insured all my children."

"The way I look on it is this," said Mrs. Kemp—"wotever yer do when they're alive, an' we all know as children is very tryin' sometimes, you should give them a good funeral when they dies. Thet's my motto, an' I've always acted up to it."

"Do you deal with Mr. Stearman?" asked Mrs. Hodges.

"No, Mrs. 'Odges, for undertikin' give me Mr. Footley every time. In the black line 'e's fust an' the rest nowhere!"

"Well, thet's very strange now—thet's just wot I think. Mr. Footley does 'is work well, an' 'e's very reasonable. I'm a very old customer of 'is, an' 'e lets me 'ave things as cheap as anybody."

"Does 'e indeed! Well, Mrs. 'Odges, if it ain't askin' too much of yer, I should look upon it as very kind if you'd go an' mike the arrangements for Liza."

"Why, certainly, Mrs. Kemp. I'm always willin' ter do a good turn to anybody, if I can."

"I want it done very respectable," said Mrs. Kemp; "I'm not goin' ter stint for nothin' for my daughter's funeral. I like plumes, you know, although they is a bit extra."

"Never you fear, Mrs. Kemp, it shall be done as well as if it was for my own 'usbind, an' I can't say more than thet. Mr. Footley thinks a deal of me, 'e does! Why, only the other dy as I was goin' inter 'is shop, 'e says, 'Good mornin', Mrs. 'Odges.' 'Good mornin', Mr. Footley,' says I. 'You've jest come in the nick of time,' says 'e. 'This gentleman an' myself,' pointin' to another gentleman as was standin' there, 'we was 'avin' a bit of an argument. Now you're a very intelligent woman, Mrs. 'Odges, and a good customer too.' 'I can say thet for myself,' says I, 'I gives yer all the work I can.' 'I believe you,' says 'e. 'Well,' 'e says, 'now which do you think? Does hoak look better than helm, or does helm look better than hoak? Hoak *versus* helm, thet's the question.' 'Well, Mr.

135

Footley,' says I, 'for my own private opinion, when you've got a nice brass plite in the middle, an' nice brass 'andles each end, there's nothin' like hoak.' 'Quite right,' says 'e, 'thet's wot I think; for coffins give me hoak any day, an' I 'ope,' says 'e, 'when the Lord sees fit ter call me to 'Imself, I shall be put in a hoak coffin myself.' 'Amen,' says I."

"I like hoak," said Mrs. Kemp. "My poor 'usbind 'e 'ad a hoak coffin. We did 'ave a job with 'im, I can tell yer. You know 'e 'ad dropsy, an' 'e swell up—oh, 'e did swell; 'is own mother wouldn't 'ave known 'im. Why, 'is leg swell up till it was as big round as 'is body, swop me bob, it did."

"Did it indeed!" ejaculated Mrs. Hodges.

"Yus, an' when 'e died they sent the coffin up. I didn't 'ave Mr. Footley at thet time; we didn't live 'ere then, we lived in Battersea, an' all our undertikin' was done by Mr. Brownin'; well, 'e sent the coffin up, an' we got my old man in, but we couldn't get the lid down, he was so swell up. Well, Mr. Brownin', 'e was a great big man, thirteen stone if 'e was a ounce. Well, 'e stood on the coffin, an' a young man 'e 'ad with 'im stood on it too, an' the lid simply wouldn't go dahn; so Mr. Brownin', 'e said, 'Jump on, missus,' so I was in my widow's weeds, yer know, but we 'ad ter get it dahn, so I stood on it, an' we all jumped, an' at last we got it to, an' screwed it; but, lor', we did 'ave a job; I shall never forget it."

Then all was silence. And a heaviness seemed to fill the air like a grey blight, cold and suffocating; and the heaviness was Death. They felt the presence in the room, and they dared not move, they dared not draw their breath. The silence was terrifying.

Suddenly a sound was heard—a loud rattle. It was from

136

the bed and rang through the room, piercing the stillness.

The doctor opened one of Liza's eyes and touched it, then he laid on her breast the hand he had been holding, and drew the sheet over her head.

Jim turned away with a look of intense weariness on his face, and the two women began weeping silently. The darkness was sinking before the day, and a dim, grey light came through the window. The lamp spluttered out.

W. Somerset Maugham

The Collected Edition

1 LIZA OF LAMBETH
2 OF HUMAN BONDAGE
3 THE MOON AND SIXPENCE
4 THE PAINTED VEIL
5 ASHENDEN
6 CAKES AND ALE
7 THE NARROW CORNER
8 DON FERNANDO
9 THEATRE
10 THE SUMMING UP
11 CHRISTMAS HOLIDAY
12 THE RAZORS EDGE
13 CREATURES OF CIRCUMSTANCE
14 CATALINA
15 A WRITER'S NOTEBOOK
16 THE TREMBLING OF A LEAF
17 ON A CHINESE SCREEN
18 THE CASUARINA TREE
19 AH KING
20 MRS. CRADDOCK
21 THE MAGICIAN
22 THEN AND NOW
23 UP AT THE VILLA
24 THE EXPLORER
25 THE MERRY-GO-ROUND